2050: India Turns 100

VAIBHAV

NOTION PRESS

NOTION PRESS

India. Singapore. Malaysia.

ISBN 979-8-893223-75-0

I dedicate this book to:

To the eternal time (kaal काल), for (only) it knows when the visions mentioned in this book will happen.

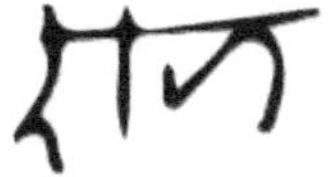

Table of Contents

Preface

After my spiritual initiation in the year 2020-21, I got inspiration to write. I got an opportunity to pen thoughts about our country, which took form of a book "Discovery of New India", published in 2021. That book discussed some problems which were introduced during the British period; and it mentioned the solutions for many of those problems.

Motivated by the observations that many suggestions and solutions mentioned in that book are actually happening in our country, I am inspired to write again.

I am writing this book, "2050 - India turns 100", from a spiritual perspective. I am observing the events in India, and in the world, from that perspective. "Seeing" the solutions for some of the toughest of the problems lingering around for over a millennium.

I am not sure if these visions are intuitions, pseudo-intuitions, my imaginations or logical conclusions of my rational mind or if these are simply wishes. However, by God's will I am inspired to write, with an intrinsic wish to see them come true in my lifetime. That's the reason I dedicate this book to time (काल) as only it knows what is there for us in the future. You will see on the dedication page, there is a handwritten Ram (राम); this is from Neeb Karori baba or Maharaj ji.

The book is staged in the year 2050. I am describing the changes that have happened between 2024-2050. The changes are in the fields of education, governance and administration model, socio-economic and cultural fabric, a transformation in India which happened after self and God realization of the masses. Believe me, the changes are radical!

The achievement lies in the acceptance of Indic wisdom by India and others. The approach anchors on the fundamental Indian wisdom of aham brahmasmi (अहं ब्रह्माऽस्मि - 'मैं ब्रह्म हूं), and vasudhaiva kutumbakam (वसुधैव कुटुम्बकम् - सम्पूर्ण धरती परिवार है).

The chapter 'Thank You Kashmir' is a special one. How does Kashmir serve as the focal point for resolving some of the toughest problems of the world? The Middle East regional issue, East/West misalignment, Communism?

What led to the spiritual reunion of the East/West? How were Lamas, and the Vatican involved in that reunion? This chapter and the Endnotes (spiritual notes) show the remarkable similarity of teachings of various religions, faiths and spiritual leaders. All converge to the fundamental truth, that the Creator is One!

Take a pause, and let's understand - once this realization is achieved it will be the Grand Unification.

The further chapters depict the world's journey for making such realizations, the intrinsic power of these realizations, and how people/countries shed the guilt of centuries or millennia after such realizations? You may wonder what was the biggest sin of the last few millennia? What is the original sin? The one that is told often or something else?

The book mentions the prominent "apologies" which some countries or regions made during these years, and more importantly why they made so?

Have you ever wondered why Kashmir's Shankaracharya hill, discovered by Adi Shankaracharya around 500 BCE, is called Solomon hill by the Jews and Christians? Why do the Muslims call it Takht-i-Sulaiman? Perhaps it is a very high spiritual place just like Kailash. Sri Aurobindo also experienced its power on his maiden visit in 1903.

The book hints on the "lost years" for the progress of India. Since the end of the Mahabharata war, the decline of human consciousness continues. When river Saraswati was asked to change its course, and go underground, as per the tale of Mahabharatha we hear from childhood, India has observed the decline.

Time tried to upturn this decline during the period 600-500 BCE when Vardhaman Mahavir, Gautam Budhha, and Adi Shankaracharya came for revival of righteousness. Time has tried to upturn the decline many times in the later periods, however the decline of India continued.

I wonder if this decline is due to declining awareness of Self, or declining realization of the absolute truth, or getting entangled (superficially) in the rituals, or due to the misunderstood meaning of chatur-varna system, and due to the growing rigidity in the socio-cultural fabric of the sub continent?

Ancient Indian consciousness declined and underwent 1000-1500 years of punishment. It deviated from its duty to remain the guiding light for the world. However, after touching the lowest level in 1857, an upturn happened in the year 1893.

The upward journey continues; and perhaps the 21st century is going to become India's century.

India should not be elated, or get flattered by this thought that the developed world has started looking at it again. It should not deviate from its duty to be the guiding light for the world.

One of my personal spiritual experiences is also the motivating factor to write this book. A question was in my mind for the last couple of years; it used to hit me like a flash many times. It is about the relationship that immortal Mahaavtar babaji holds with Jesus Christ. Both came on earth around 2000 years back, and both are revered as highly spiritual God realized souls. I always had the intuition they are the same (one soul), but haven't heard of it from any credible source. With that question I went to the YSS Ashram in Dwarahat in Uttarakhand on Christmas eve 2023.

Next morning we had planned to visit the famous cave of Mahaavtar babaji. During the Christmas eve meditation at the ashram, I repeated my question again. I heard the inner voice "that's the reason you are called here on Christmas"!

Vaibhav

Meerut, August 2024

1 The Bench

Today is the first day of the new year 2050. I am in Rishikesh sitting on an iron bench at the banks of river Ganga (Ganges). This bench has been here for many years, in fact, decades. People who come to take a stroll in the mornings or evenings at the banks of the river prefer to sit quietly on this bench, perhaps to retrospect about their life or simply observe nature or perhaps do nothing.

Near this bench has been the Swami Rama Sadhana Mandir Ashram for almost 90 years now. People who visit this Ashram on the banks of river Ganga, often continue their sadhana on this old bench. Opposite to the ashram, is AIIMS Rishikesh. Many attendants, friends & relatives of the patients come here for relaxing short walks along the Ganga waters. The local residents, who are staying here for decades, have grown old with this bench. They come here especially in mornings and evenings and in the afternoons of winters. My small hut or hermitage, as I call it, is nearby. It is a tiny apartment, just big enough for me and my family when we visit here. Whenever I get time, from grand parenting, I come to Rishikesh to reconnect with nature, to explore and expand my inner Self. Many times, my wife jokingly says, when will your exploration of Self get over?

Today the world is entering into a special year, 2050. For almost 30 years, there have been lots of forecasts, if not prophecies, for this year. I would prefer to call those as wishes.

Like all countries, India has been waiting to see the light of 1st January 2050. Just a few years ago, it turned 100, i.e. it completed its 100 years of independence from the British Raj. Lots has changed in these 100 years; much has changed in the last 50 years specially. I have been a quiet witness to those changes, subtle or gross (or even crude) being more than 70 years old now. A long list of changes, indeed!

Across the Ganga waters, I see a herd (family) of elephants strolling at the foothills of the small hillock. Their routine is to come to the river every morning and evening, to drink water, bathe, play and have fun.

Nothing seems to have changed for them in the last few decades. Their days are almost the same, aligned with nature, vegetation, and weather patterns. They are always together, always connected to mother nature, to their habitat, and perhaps with their inner Selves. Perhaps, they are not as exploratory as the humans who take different paths to lead life. I wonder if these creatures have the slightest idea how complex a human life is! Or if I can dare to say, how complex we make our life which is otherwise much simpler!

We often need props, anchors or guides to know the purpose of our life. In fact, not all are fortunate enough to realise the purpose of their lives at the early stage; some leave the world without knowing the true purpose of their lives. At times, their last years are quite lonely, helpless and painful.

This bench is freshly painted green. Perhaps a day or two before to welcome the new year with a fresh look. However, I could feel the same old metallic projection pressing on my back. It has been doing its job, sincerely, for almost 30 years. It was in 2021 when I discovered this bench on my maiden visit to this place. Perhaps, this small projection on this bench is a reminder for me to remain grounded. I agree with that anonymous saint who has said that certain aspects of life do not change! This metallic projection is one of such constants in my life.

Today being the first day of the new year, is a special one. Scores of people are walking along the banks of river Ganga. It is a sunny but cold afternoon. They are wearing all sorts of caps. The different designs and colours of their caps represent the rich diversity of our country. Since ancient times, the uniqueness of our country lies in its cultural diversity integrated beautifully into its social fabric. The land where the taste of ground water and dialect change every few hundred miles, the land knitted by the cultural threads starting from the beautiful eastern states fed by mighty river Brahmaputra to the white and golden sands of the west, by the threads spanning from the mystic northern Himalayas to the culturally rich states of the south overseeing the great Indian ocean. Such is the diverse geographical span of this ancient country.

I am now in my 70s, sitting here in the retrospective. I am getting hundreds of vivid memories, clear flashes of the past happenings and events that happened to me, to my people, to my country, to the world in the last 40-50 years. India has come quite far on the path of true progress. In fact, the whole world has made significant progress, it has come quite closer not just physically, as some regions reunited culturally, but spiritually.

Post the covid-19 pandemic, which shook the world during the years 2020-22, many regions came closer to each other, especially the ones which shared a common history, or had similar cultural values. Cultural rearrangement happened in the Indian subcontinent, in the south-east asian countries (ASEAN countries). Fragmentations and rearrangements happened in China and Tibet. Russia and Europe aligned more, miracles happened in the middle east, and cultural rearrangements happened in the African union as well.

The 21st century modern world made significant progress in establishing harmony among many nations, religions and cultures. By the time the United Nations turned 100, in the year 2045, it had achieved a lot on its charter.

How did it happen?

Over the last 30 years, the most influential of the world realised that the race to reach the top never ends. I recall how the pandemic brought the so-called most powerful countries to their knees. Those powerful countries had realised during the pandemic waves that humans ought to respect mother nature.

I wonder that not very long ago India gave this message to the world "Vasudhaiva Kutumbakam" meaning all His creations are one family. It was a Global 20 event hosted by India in the year 2023, when India had given this message "One Earth, One Family, One Future". The message struck the right chords, at the right time. It gave a new direction, a fresh guidance (a new mantra) to the world recovering from the devastation caused by the covid-19 pandemic.

After the G20 event in 2023, the world leaders who happened to be the change makers of the world, understood this universal message of well being and coexistence of all. In the next 2 decades, countries worked together, took significant steps to achieve the same. The message holds the power to change the perspective of looking at the world, looking at the natural resources, looking at the natural creations, looking at the living beings, looking at the non-living aspects of the Mother Earth, thereby it changed the perspectives and weightages for good.

The world gained a fresh outlook, a fresh perspective, a new zeal to live together a life of harmony, gratitude and mutual respect. The message held the power to eradicate many ailments of the society, not limited discriminations and racism. While there were conflicts in many regions of the world during the last 30 years, those remain largely localised. In most of the cases, there was no mad rush of fighting "together as alliances" in order to scale up wars or to mint money from it. Hence, the scale of those wars, thankfully, remained localised in most of the cases.

One Earth, One Family, One Future became a universal message, and slowly all the countries got aligned to it.

Vasudhaiva Kutumbakum, is a timeless truth, realised and developed by the ancient rishis and spiritual leaders of the region. This universal message, given by the God realised and Self realised saints of India, has served as the guide to the modern world. It showed the path of harmonious co-living, living with self respect, living in harmony with mother nature, and how to live a purposeful life.

As we are entering into 2050, I am not exaggerating the guidance which the world countries received from ancient wisdom of India. Now India is seen as a friend of all (Vishwa Mitra). Many now think that India will (soon) become the spiritual leader of the world (Vishva Guru), as was foreseen by the enlightened people of the last two centuries, the 20th century and the 19th century. Modern rishis like Swami Vivekananda, Sri Aurobindo, Paramahansa Yogananda, and many of their God realised contemporaries foretold it. The visions, the prophecies of those God realised souls, near avatars, have been realised to a great extent with global acceptance. Countries now look upon India in finding holistic solutions for nearly all the issues and problems concerning nature and its resources.

The UN and all member countries have understood the meaning of true progress, we all understand the difference between the need and greed. We have understood that material progress cannot bring content, harmony and solace throughout the world. Firstly because material progress cannot happen uniformly across the world. Secondly, not everyone, not every culture of the world gets inspired merely by material progress.

Looking around to see for ourselves, many regions and cultures of the world are happy living a simple life in the lap of mother nature, living a peaceful, non polluted life with the meagre (minimal) belongings which they received from their forefathers. Imposing the material progress as the true progress, that idea was shunned by the countries of the world. When the UN turned 100, it was established that the countries and cultures should have complete freedom in defining the true progress, as per the indigenous thoughts and cultural values of the region.

Big Daddy or the bully nations, no more impose their perspectives on the entire world. For this United Nations, and the associated bodies played a significant role with appreciable contribution from India. There has been good progress across the world. For example, poverty has been eradicated across the globe, initially by the redistribution of wealth and thereafter by the holistic policies and good governance of the countries of the world. Now every family lives a respectful life and they have the required resources available for them.

I recall reading a book titled Ignited Minds by Dr. APJ Abdul Kalam, who was a prominent scientist and served as the president of India. In his book Dr. Kalam defined poverty as the biggest problem for our country. There were many reasons he had given to conclude this point. When I read his book first in 2020, I had agreed to it and today when poverty has been eradicated by the conscious measures taken collectively by the countries, I see that it actually has eradicated lots of social and mental ailments.

Only a well fed body and morally educated mind can bring true progress and prosperity in the society. This is as clear as the Ganga flowing in front of me.

The sun is about to settle down now. It's getting colder, and is about 10 degrees centigrade. The elephant herd across the river is getting ready to go back into the jungle, which is on the other side of the hillock. Perhaps it is time for me to go back to my hermitage and make some new year wish calls to my family and friends.

2 Prabhu Shri Ram

I got up earlier than usual today. I feel more energetic, perhaps because it's 22 January today. Since the year 2024, this day has been celebrated as the second coming of Prabhu Shri Ram. Shri Ram has been *aradhya* of billions of people across millennia. I came closer to Him in the year 2020, the year which shocked the modern world by the covid-19 pandemic. It was during those infamous lock downs I saw the TV serial Ramayana for the second time in my life. It had a deep impact and turned me towards spirituality.

Recalling the personal experiences that followed the year 2020, I got ready for the walk towards my bench (my Bodhi tree), at the banks of river Ganga in Rishikesh. While walking along the banks of Ganga I noticed the river is more vibrant and noisy today. The chirps of the birds around me are louder than usual for this time of the day. Perhaps the birds are jovial like me as if celebrating and singing for Prabhu Shri Ram.

I sank into my bench, closed my eyes and started recollecting memories of the last 30 years or so. The clear visions for the 22nd January 2024 started rolling over. Perhaps the timewheel (the kaal chakra) changed for the good of the world on that day. That day onwards the heavens with all their divine forces reestablished the divinity in the Earth's atmosphere and on the surface of the Earth. The aura of Prabhu Shri Ram was reestablished, in His consecrated idol. The divine light, which is the source of divinity, knowledge and spiritual progress, mentioned in the spiritual books of all religions of the world, that divinity touched the Earth's surface on that day. The touch was soft and subtle. In the years that followed, many beings on this planet got touched and charged from this divinity, either being aware of it or not.

The river Ganga flowing in front of me, is as if saying that *on this day I am most cheerful and playful.* The way Shri Ram descended on the earth for the second time holds the same divinity as the day when one of

His forefathers Raja Bhagirath brought me on this earth from the heavens for this part of the world. Ma Ganga continues to say, he brought my descent with this tapas and Bhagirath Prayas. With the help and blessings from *bhole* shankar Shiv ji my strong and mighty descent was controlled. However, the second descent of Prabhu Shri Ram in the year 2024 was the most soft and subtle descent that a God could make, as if to say to the people gently "do not worry, I am here".

Many people acknowledge that the last 25 years have brought a positive change in their lives and in the world. People started respecting the other beings around them, more than ever. People became more open to the new ideas, they became more flexible towards other people's religious beliefs and practices. They became more understanding and helped each other in times of need. The people of the world, especially the religious leaders of all the religions of the world, could see the commonality among all the religions with their own personal divine experiences. They could see and realise that all paths lead to the same source, the supreme source, the Supreme Creator.

The Supreme Soul, given different names by different regions and religions, like Ishwar, Allah, Ik Onkar, God, Parampita, Waheguru, Jina, and likewise. This realisation was instrumental to bring a radical shift in the thinking of the masses, their attitude towards the others. First, the religious leaders realised the oneness of the Supreme, then the influential and powerful of those times realised by their own experiences, realisations and visions, that all paths lead to one. Those paths differ only in practices, names and beliefs which evolved over the millenia in the different regions and cultures of the world.

This mega realisation brought immense harmony, peace, prevented and resolved many power struggles, religious and ethnic struggles across the world. The establishment of Prabhu Shri Ram temple in Ayodhya, drew millions and billions towards spirituality and reestablished respect for ancient Indian and ancient Asian values and wisdom. Irrespective of their religion or faith, more people understand Shri Ram, his life events, and are drawn towards his qualities and the qualities of his contemporaries. People of today's modern world find role models and guides in Him and in many of his contemporaries. Perhaps their true aspiration for acquiring the *gunas* or qualities and attributes from His life is more developed now.

This also shows that certain qualities, aspects and attributes do not change with the passage of time. These are timeless and immortal. These remain constant in spite of the lapse of time, in spite of change of place or space and in spite of the change in context or situation. True human aspirations / inspirations do not change with the change of the priorities or the world order or the living conditions. The qualities which are fundamental and dear to human nature remain as is.

With such a diverse set of characters available in the divine characters of Ramayana, people tend to find some who are more close to them, they seek to align more with them, become more like them, be one with them. This is the true seeking, in this process of aspiration and devoted efforts, they make progress, evolve and finally, move closer to the infinite.

Sitting on this bench watching the cheerful flow of Ganga, listening to loud chirping of birds, observing scores of people strolling on the riverbank, I am wondering about the miracles that have happened on this earth after that consecration in the year 2024. Maryada Purushottam Prabhu Shri Ram is the one having all of the 16 gunas - the 16 qualities needed for a perfect human being. In Puranas, Prabhu Shri Ram is worshipped by all the Gods and Goddesses. His second coming established a new anchor or *aadhaar* or axis or *dhuri* for the Indian masses to seek to discover their lives' purpose and act on the principles of *dharma*, love, compassion, harmony and respect for all. That is the sincere adoption of the message Vasudhaiva Kutumbakam.

Maryada Purushottam Shri Ram's life events teach us the deep meanings of living in a maryada, i.e. in dharmic limits or universal defined boundaries. These dharmic boundaries were evolved and developed by numerous ancient seers and saints, God realised men and women of ancient India. His life events teach living within those maryadas from the perspective of a disciple, a son, a brother, a husband, a father, a friend, a master, a wanderer, a warrior, a saviour, even an opponent, and many other high human values acceptable for the Indian cultural ethos. That is the reason He is known as Purushottam or Purushottama, meaning the most perfect human being.

From the Ramayana, we know about the life full of hardships of Shri Ram and Mata Sita. There are certain aspects of His life, which remind me of the power of living in maryada or restraint. When Rishi Vishwamitra had taken Shri Ram and Shri Lakshaman to his ashram, to make it free from the demons, especially Tarka, it is said that Shri Ram did not shoot an arrow on her as she was in feminine form. Such is the greatness and gentleness of His nature. However, as she was at that moment, representing the demonic *asuric* shakti, which was to be put to rest for the benefit of the human race, Shri Ram killed her based upon his wisdom.

On one other occasion when Shri Ram had reached the southernmost tip of the Indian mainland, he prayed to the vast sea in front, requesting it to give them a way for Lanka. Shri Ram who was equipped with the most powerful divine weapons from Rishi Vashitha, Rishi Vishwamitra, Rishi Augustya, did not show his powers to the defiant sea. It was only after a long wait and no answer for his prayers, He showed the glimpse of his power. Even in the battle with Ravan, Shri Ram restrained from using the most destructive weapons given to him by the sages and Gods as those could impact the others for a long time. That was the maryada, a self imposed boundary he showed even in the most difficult times of his life.

When I recount the love and compassion He had for other beings and nature, some incidents always stand above all. The love and compassion He had for Jatayu, the love He had for Sabri Ma, the love He showed to his injured Vaanar sena, the love, compassion and respect He had for even the smallest beings, the love He had for his father, mothers, brothers, Sita ma, Hanuman ji move me.

It is said that when Shri Ram came to know of the dilemma of his father, Maharaj Dashrath - the dilemma of choosing between his promise to fulfil his wife's wish Kaikeyi which was in contrast to his own wish to coronate Shri Ram, Shri Ram being the most loving, caring, and respecting son relieved his father from that dilemma. Shri Ram told Maharaj, His father, that He is leaving the throne on his own and is going to exile by his own will. Thus saving his father from the immense pain of sending Him off to exile.

Another instance which inspires me a lot is when Shri Ram was asked to shoot an arrow, piercing Ravan's heart during the Lanka war. He said he won't do it, because Janaki lives in Ravan's heart as well, thus He cannot see her in pain even in His opponent's heart. That is the tender love Shri Ram has for Ma Sita, Janaki.

Since the year 2024, the aura of Prabhu Shri Ram has been inspiring and motivating millions and billions of people on this earth, irrespective of their religious beliefs or the geographical boundaries. They respect him, pray to him, follow him for the noble virtues he carries. Shri Ram is everyone's, He is the noblest king which this subcontinent has seen. Shri Ram is past, present and future. Sri Ram is infinite.

3 Thank you Kashmir

Especially in the last 20 years the Indian subcontinent and adjoining ASEAN countries have seen a stronger bond among each other. These countries, some of which were opponents for decades, have been inspired from the rise of Indian thought of oneness - Indian thought of unity, love and compassion among all the beings in nature. They are aligned with the Indian way of living and co-living, and value Indian culture more than ever now. It may be appropriate to say that just like in history when Indian culture, thought of oneness, knowledge, way of living was prevalent in most of South Asia, the same is being observed again. Nations are more united now than ever in modern history on the principles of healthy coexistence, mutual respect, mutual cooperation and mutual collaboration for the utilisation of natural resources and for resolving the environmental issues.

Yoga, meditation and Shri Ram's aura have brought the world together. Some miracles have led to this state of the modern world in such a short span of two decades. Firstly, religious leaders and people of different beliefs have reported seeing visions or hearing voices of their Angels, Avatars, Messengers, Gurus and God. Initially very few spoke of it openly, however later on many have reported such sights and hearings. Muslims have reported seeing Prophet Muhammad in their dreams in which the Prophet repeated his earliest teachings which were marked by his insistence on the oneness of God. The primary message of Islam is the belief in the oneness of God (Allah). Christians have reported Jesus Christ appearing in their dreams. His teachings revolve around themes of oneness of God, love, compassion, forgiveness, humility, and service. Jesus said God is one and he is the most merciful.

Of the Indigenous religions of India - Sanatan Dharm (Hindus), Sikhs fundamentally are monotheistic, though they appear as polytheistic; however, the various gods and goddesses are viewed strictly as embodiments of the Divine Brahman, Wahe Guru or Supreme soul, and so the system is monotheistic. Jainism and Buddhism are non-theistic religions (no belief in a creator God), however Jains believe in

Devas, and Tirthankars (highest saints). Indigenous religions or sects practising people have reported seeing Shri Ram, Shri Krishna, Devi ma, Guru Nanak dev ji, Bhagwan Mahavir, Gautam Budhha, other *bhagwaans* in their dreams or in contemplation or during meditation or dhyana.

Likewise, people across the world have reported seeing visions or hearing voices of the angels, of the prophets, of the ancient rishis and gurus, spirits, and spiritual guides quite frequently in the last two decades. The common message which they are receiving from these visions and voices is that all creations are one and those are created by one supreme soul, a formless Supreme Power which different people call differently as Ishwar or Allah or Ik Onkar or Wahe Guru, God or Jina, or Parameshwara. He manifests into various forms at different times of need, in different regions of the world, as Messenger of God, Son of God, Avtar, Spiritual guide, Saint or Sufi, Guru or a spiritual teacher.

These voices and visions have a miraculous impact on the perceptions of billions of people. The task that was otherwise impossible for the humans to achieve, has been done so easily by the creator Himself. These visions and voices instructed all, that the time has come to see the oneness behind all of forms and accept the oneness of His creations, continue the good practices developed by various belief systems (religions or sects or regions), shed the ones which trouble or exploit others, don't impose the greatness of one belief system on the other. These religions are like the fingers of the hand. Every finger is needed. Initially these visions were ignored as false dreams or hallucinations, however when many experienced people collectively realised that these are the Godly instructions meant for the modern world.

There were certain events which happened post the year 2024 which changed the entire world for good. For example, the much talked about the missing years of Jesus Christ were researched extensively, by many governments, historians to know where Jesus Christ was staying from the age of 13 to 29. And then later on after the age of 33 till He left his body for heaven to be with His father. This research was a pressing need of the 21st century as there were many claims, for over a century, that as a teenager Jesus travelled through the old silk route and reached the ancient Indian subcontinent. The research was supported by various governments, including India and the Vatican because the idea was to see, to discover the ways to unite the east and the west for good.

The Dalai Lama supported the availability and translations of the ancient Tibetian texts which mentioned Jesus's travels in India and Tibet. Artificial Intelligence played a key role in the translations, and reconciliations of the ancient texts. These researches were carried out for a decade, debated and deliberated by the church, governments, religious leaders and powerful lobbyists and even atheists of the world. Ultimately, the common findings were accepted for the true unification of the modern world.

It was thus established that Jesus Christ had travelled to India as a teenager and had learned the techniques of yoga, meditation, self healing, and other eastern philosophies from the saints, rishis and gurus of various prominent religions prevalent in India in those times, namely, Jainism, Buddhism, and Sanatan Dharma (which is Hinduism). He gathered spiritual knowledge, wisdom, attained enlightenment and realised that He is Son of God. His route was traced from the Northwest India frontier, the current day Afghanistan, Pakistan, to Rajasthan, Gujarat, on the west, to Jagannath Puri in the east, thereafter to Kashi which is Banaras or Varanasi in the north, to Nepal, Kashmir, and Tibet.

In India Jesus acquired enlightenment and became God realised. He realised that He is God sent, an avatar, Son of God or Ishwar taken incarnation at that time for spreading and rekindling the love, compassion and harmony to his fellow countrymen, to the regions where He belonged - the Arabic region. Jesus, or Isa Massih went back to his homeland Jerusalem, in the Arab region and preached to the people there. Jesus preached with love and compassion and healed their souls and bodies through miraculous touch. Certain people felt jealous, insecure and they could not align with his spiritual powers, his teachings and thus conspired against Him and crucified Him.

We all believe that Jesus came back to life on the day of Easter. It was a general opinion that after the resurrection, He left for heaven (ascension). During the research it was established that Jesus Christ, who is an avatar who had borne the physical pain, went into the state of samadhi (deep meditation) on the holy cross. After the resurrection, he decided to leave his region along with his family and followers, with a promise to come back.

The results of the research established that while on the way back from Jerusalem to Kashmir, mother Mary (or Maryam) left for heavenly abode at a place called Murree (in Pakistan). Isa Masih or Jesus Christ made Kashmir as His new home and lived here forever. Rozabal is a shrine located in the Khanyar quarter in the downtown area of Srinagar in Kashmir. The word roza means tomb, the word bal means place. Locals believe a Jewish sage is buried here, Yuz Asaf or Isa Masih, alongside another Muslim holy man, Mir Sayyid Naseeruddin.

It is important to note that the three major conflicts troubling the world for many centuries got resolved between 2030 and 2050. Ironically, the solution was found in the history of Kashmir.

Firstly, when this fact was established, Jesus (Isa Masih) lived in Kashmir for the rest of His human life, along with His followers, to spread love and compassion in the region. The general acceptance of this fact brought the west closer to the east (India). This united the spiritual people among Christians and Indians to the core, as they found a common past.

Secondly, the Jews descendents who are mostly practising Muslims, are living in Kashmir. They are the examples of living and practising Musalmans who have high regards for their Jewish roots. The envoy of these people met the influential religious leaders of Jews and Muslims, and with years of effort, they were able to reconcile the fundamental differences between the Jews and Muslims of the Arabic region.

The third issue which was kind-of sorted by Kashmir and Ladakh, was the end of communist China's subjugation of Tibet. Communism was distorted in practice by the erstwhile USSR then later on by the Republic of China, and some other countries like

Korea (N). Communism lost its hold in Asia. After the year 2030, people of China realised that an (imperfect) human being can neither take the place of God nor take the place of an enlightened soul (Spiritual master). Hence an imperfect man cannot be blindly followed. People realised that even the best among the human leaders behaves differently and takes different decisions in similar situations. They cannot remain loyal and aligned to such a leader. They rejected the idea of communism in China. By the time independent India turned 100 and China turned 99 Communism was gone forever from that land.

Kashmiri Muslims apologised for the exodus of Kashmiri Hindus. The exodus that occurred in Kashmir refers to the forced displacement of the Kashmiri Pandit community from the Kashmir valley in the late 1980s and early 1990s; this issue was hurting the national sentiments for decades.

The modern world remains indebted to Kashmir, which is historically the land of Rishi Kashyap as per the Indian belief. He is one of the Saptarishis, the seven ancient sages of the Rigveda. Rishi Kashyap is the most ancient and venerated rishi, along with the other Saptarishis, listed in the Brihadaranyaka Upanishad.

With the traditional seat of Ma Saraswati (Ma Sharda, a form of Shakti) and Kailash (seat of Shiva) on its east, Kashmir became the spiritual centre of the world. There are four or five edges of Mount Kailash which point towards Kashi in the southeast, Mahakaleshwar (*Kaal*) in the southwest, Kashmir in the northwest and the two edges of north and northeast point towards the erstwhile (K)Communist China and Korea. In these last two decades, Mount Kailash has played its role in setting things right and harmonised on the face of the earth.

Three major conflicts troubling the world for many centuries got resolved between 2030 and 2050. The solution was found in the history of Kashmir. I must say, Thank you Kashmir.

4 (2047) India Turns 100

Since ancient times, India's influence on the world has been profound. Legends speak of noble kings who once ruled the subcontinent with justice, valour, wisdom and benevolence. Our Puranas tell of the immortal King Mahabali, reigning in what is now Kerala, affectionately known as "God's own country." It is said that Mahabali's dominion stretched across the known world, even reaching into the heavens. Similarly, the epic journey of Shri Ram traversed the length and breadth of India, establishing the righteous rule of Rama Rajya, showcasing how virtue can endure even in the harshest trials.

Ramayana, in its various interpretations, reverberates throughout South Asia, embodying timeless ideals. Likewise, the epic Mahabharat depicts the scale and span of the sub-continent in those times. The Tale of Shri Krishna unveils the challenges faced by ancient Indian rulers, encountering kings from distant lands like Yunnan, what we now know as Greece, as exemplified by the enigmatic Kalyavan (कालयवन), an invincible king born from Indian parents. These interactions, often overlooked in discussions of Indian, Indo-European, or Indo-Greek history, represent a crucial aspect of our shared heritage.

In my recollection of the years around 2030, emerged a significant moral and historical renaissance, offering a much-needed morale boost and a corrective lens on our collective past.

A pivotal historical correction overturned centuries-old misconceptions, revealing that Alexander, also known as Sikander, did not defeat Indian king Porus or Puru in 326 BCE. Instead, he retreated to Greece via a different route, preserving his reputation after facing formidable opposition from Puru. This revelation shattered the notion of his invincibility, as he was compelled to leave India without achieving conquest. This correction emerged about a century after Sri Aurobindo's debunking of the Aryan invasion theory, which was propagated by the British to subjugate Indian thought.

Between the reign of Chandra Gupta Maurya and the ascendancy of the Mughals, India witnessed significant shifts in power, including the rule of the prosperous Guptas, great Cholas, Cheras, Pandyas, Rashtrakutas, Pallavas, Bhoj, Vijayanagara kings, etc followed by courageous Marathas, Sikhs and the indomitable Rajputs, Jats, and Ahoms. Collaboration and treaties shaped the landscape, leading to a fragmented yet resilient nation.

The scars of the 1857 uprising, India's first war of independence against the British, gradually transformed into a spiritual resurgence, culminating in the pivotal year of 1893. This year marked a turning point as India embarked on its journey into the 20th century, fueled by a renewed sense of identity and purpose.

In the transformative year of 1893, a significant union between East and West began to unfold. Swami Vivekananda embarked on a journey to America, participating in the World's Parliament of Religions in Chicago, while Sri Aurobindo returned to India after his 14-year study (which he jokingly called exile) in Britain, arriving in Baroda. Concurrently, in Gorakhpur, a child was born under the grace of the immortal spiritual master Maha Avatar Baba Ji, destined to become Paramahansa Yogananda, a revered spiritual leader who would later spend over three decades in America, guiding its inhabitants towards spiritual enlightenment.

The visits of Swami Vivekananda and Paramhansa Yogananda initiated a spiritual awakening in America, igniting a thirst for Eastern wisdom that reverberated throughout the 20th century and beyond. Paramhansa Yogananda's seminal work, "Autobiography of a Yogi," continues to inspire millions, embodying the timeless truths of spirituality for more than 100 years.

Recent history underscores the transformative power of acknowledging past mistakes. Countries like Japan and Germany, confronting their roles in World War II atrocities, emerged from the shadows of guilt to achieve remarkable progress. Similarly, Italy disavowed its fascist past, embracing a new trajectory of growth and prosperity.

Similarly, India began to confront its past, particularly after 2020, by rejecting the legacy of pseudo-Gandhian figures and embracing the true spirit of its independence movement. The nation honoured its freedom fighters and distilled the essential values of its leaders. The awakening of the populace revealed decades of deception, prompting a collective resolve for change. India embraced a newfound reverence for its freedom fighters, recognizing their pivotal role in liberating the nation from British rule in 1947.

From these leaders, valuable qualities were distilled: Mahatma Gandhi's emphasis on self-restraint and cleanliness, envisioning Ramrajya; Dr. Ambedkar's advocacy for equality and justice; and Netaji Subhas Bose's charisma in unifying the nation and reigniting motivation. These attributes formed the bedrock of modern India, blending tradition with progress. The integrated India of today stands as a testament to the sacrifices and guidance of countless luminaries who shaped the trajectory of Young India in the 20th century, laying the foundation for a vibrant and democratic nation.

Yet, the vision for 21st-century India remains incomplete without the integration of its spiritual and cultural essence, passed down through millennia by ancient saints and sages like Rishi Vashisht, Vishwamitra, Valmiki, Agastya, and Vyasa. In the luminosity of these ancient teachings, modern-day Rishis like Swami Vivekananda, Sri Aurobindo, and

Paramhansa Yogananda stand as towering figures, illuminating the path towards individual and collective enlightenment.

As we navigate the complexities of the modern world, the wisdom of these spiritual gurus serves as a guiding light, propelling India towards its destiny as a beacon of spiritual enlightenment and cultural richness. The year 1893 marked not only the convergence of great souls but also the beginning of a new chapter in India's timeless journey towards self-realization and global leadership in the pursuit of truth and righteousness.

The convergence of three modern sages in the significant year of 1893 marked a pivotal moment in India's spiritual and cultural evolution. These enlightened beings, chosen as guides and torchbearers, were entrusted with laying the foundation of the nascent nation. Alongside them stood a pantheon of revered figures, past and contemporary Rishis, and God-realized spiritual guides, including Swami Narayana, Swami Dayanand Saraswati, Shri Ramakrishna Paramhansa, Lahiri Mahashay, Neem Karoli Baba, Anandamoyi Ma, Shirdi Sai Baba, Shri Ramana Maharshi, J.

Krishnamurthi, and many others, illuminating the path for millions.

Among these luminaries, Sri Aurobindo a *trikaldarshi*, blessed with vision across time, is akin to the ancient Rishis. Sri Aurobindo who was once declared as the most dangerous freedom fighter by the British, was revered as a prominent leader of Congress from 1905 to 1909. Sri Aurobindo's wisdom was sought by luminaries like Rabindranath Tagore, Bal Gangadhar Tilak, Bipin Chandra Pal, Chitranjan Das, and other contemporaries. Netaji Subhas Chandra Bose considered him a guiding light in his pursuit of national service.

For four decades, from 1910 to 1950, Sri Aurobindo dedicated himself to elucidating India's ancient texts, philosophy, and wisdom, inspired by the divine instruction received in a divine darshan of Shri Krishna during his period in Alipore jail in 1908. Improved in spiritual practice by the spirit of Swami Vivekananda and Shri Krishna, tasked with illuminating the path of harmony, knowledge, and peaceful coexistence, Sri Aurobindo's life's work transcended the confines of conventional roles. Though offered the first Presidency of independent

India, he gracefully declined, recognizing that his mission transcended any office or title.

In the year 2022, India commemorated the 150th birth anniversary of Sri Aurobindo, dedicating the year to the dissemination of his teachings and insights. His legacy endures as a beacon of spiritual illumination, guiding India and the world towards greater understanding, harmony, and enlightenment.

In the year 2047, India introduced a significant change by instituting a new civilian award, the highest of its kind, named the Bharat Maharatna. This honour was bestowed to pay homage to six prominent figures of the 20th century, who had profoundly guided and enlightened both the people and governments of India. The inaugural recipients of the Bharat Maharatna were Mahatma Gandhi, Dr. B.R. Ambedkar, and Netaji Subhas Chandra Bose, recognized for their pivotal roles in societal integration and the upliftment of moral values. Swami Vivekananda, Sri Aurobindo, and Yogananda Paramhansa for being the spiritual guides for the country.

The enduring spirits of three enlightened figures will continue to grace us with their guidance for centuries: Swami Vivekananda, Sri Aurobindo, and Yogananda Paramhansa. Titles are superfluous for such realized souls, yet out of heartfelt respect and to seek their continued blessings, the nation united to pay homage. Thus, the people came together to offer their sincere reverence to these luminaries.

In the tapestry of India's evolution, the threads of spirituality and cultural integration are woven alongside the struggles and triumphs of countless luminaries. As India strides into the 21st century, it embraces the legacy of its past while charting a course towards a future imbued with wisdom, compassion, and enlightenment.

5 Paradigm shift in Education

In ancient India, education was imparted to make a person a good human being with a moral anchor and someone who had compassion (love) towards others, nature and nation. Dr. APJ Abdul Kalam, had mentioned in his book Ignited Minds, "*Spirituality must be integrated with education. Self-realization is the focus. Each one of us must become aware of our higher self. We are links of the great past to a grand future. We should ignite our dormant inner energy and let it guide our lives. The radiance of such minds embarked on constructive endeavour will bring peace, prosperity and bliss to this nation.*" This held the key, and was put into practice in the last 30 years.

Today, I find myself back on my bench, my own personal Bodhi tree. It's Basant Panchmi, the fifth day of the month of spring. On this auspicious day, Goddess Saraswati, also known as Shaarda Ma, is revered. Across all strata of society, people offer prayers to Goddess Saraswati, the embodiment of knowledge, wisdom, and *pragya*, seeking her guidance to steer them along the path of true progress.

Families with young children partake in a special ritual. They encourage their little ones to inscribe the sacred syllable "OM" or "AUM" or the initial syllable of their mother tongue onto rice grains, wheat flour, slates, or notebooks. This act symbolizes the blessed commencement of their journey into reading and writing, a familial tradition aimed at nurturing the child's initial steps into literacy under the benevolent gaze of Ma Saraswati.

In the 20th century, modern education placed less emphasis on sensory development, focusing instead on honing logical and analytical faculties, and prioritizing rote memorization. While this approach had its merits, it primarily served the colonial agenda of human resource development during the British Raj, valuing individuals with high intelligence quotient (IQ) and strong memory retention.

However, in the 21st century, particularly in India, educational paradigms underwent a transformation. The New Education Policy 2020 (NEP 2020) heralded a shift in focus towards personalized development, localized teaching methods, and fostering analytical skills relevant to a child's environment. By advocating teaching in the mother tongue and nurturing holistic perspectives, NEP 2020 aimed to empower students to apply knowledge effectively in real-life situations.

This fundamental shift in education levelled the playing field for the children coming from diverse socio-economic backgrounds. By embracing mother tongue instruction, children were able to comprehend better, absorb, analyze and apply knowledge, fostering practical skills over mere memorization. NEP 2020 drew inspiration from three core principles elucidated by Sri Aurobindo and The Mother in their 1920 treatise on education.

The first principle challenges conventional wisdom, asserting that nothing can be taught in the truest sense. Rather, it suggests that every child possesses innate abilities and intelligence, honed through sensory perception and logical reasoning. Given the right environment and guidance, children can organically synthesize knowledge and experience into meaningful understanding.

The second principle advocates for an inclusive and nurturing learning environment, wherein each child is encouraged to explore and question, and grow at his/her own pace. Rote memorization is eschewed in favor of fostering genuine curiosity and critical thinking, empowering students to make informed choices aligned with their passions and inclinations.

The third principle underscores the importance of using relatable examples in teaching, moving from the familiar to the abstract. Sri Aurobindo said examples should be from near to far. By contextualizing concepts within the child's immediate surroundings, educators facilitate deeper comprehension and engagement. This localized approach fosters practical understanding, enabling students to apply theoretical knowledge to real-world scenarios.

In essence, NEP 2020 embodied a paradigm shift towards holistic education, nurturing not just intellect but also emotional intelligence and practical skills. By embracing indigenous wisdom and fostering a conducive learning environment, it empowers every child to realize their full potential and contribute meaningfully to society.

Sitting on my bench, I recall the profound wisdom Sri Aurobindo and The Mother shared with the world on Child's Education. Below is the summary from Bulletin, February 1951.

The education of a human being should begin at birth and continue throughout his life. Indeed, if we want this education to have its maximum result, it should begin even before birth; in this case it is the mother herself who proceeds with this education by means of a twofold action: first, upon herself for her own improvement, and secondly, upon the child whom she is forming physically. For it is certain that the nature of the child to be born depends very much upon the mother who forms it, upon her aspiration and will as well as upon the material surroundings in which she lives.

To see that her thoughts are always beautiful and pure, her feelings always noble and fine, her material surroundings as harmonious as possible and full of a great simplicity—this is the part of education which should apply to the mother herself. And if she has in addition a conscious and definite will to form the child according to the highest ideal she can conceive, then the very best conditions will be realised so that the child can come into the world with his utmost potentialities. How many difficult efforts and useless complications would be avoided in this way!

Education to be complete must have five principal aspects corresponding to the five principal activities of the human being: the physical, the vital, the mental, the psychic and the spiritual. Usually, these phases of education follow chronologically the growth of the individual; this, however, does not mean that one of them should replace another, but that all must continue, completing one another until the end of his life.

We propose to study these five aspects of education one by one and also their interrelationships. But before we enter into the details of the subject, I wish to make a recommendation to parents. Most parents, for various reasons, give very little thought to the true education which should be imparted to children. When they have brought a child into the world, provided him with food, satisfied his various material needs and looked after his health more or less carefully, they think they have fully discharged their duty. Later on, they will send him to school and hand over to the teachers the responsibility for his education.

There are other parents who know that their children must be educated and who try to do what they can. But very few, even among those who are most serious and sincere, know that the first thing to do, in order to be able to educate a child, is to educate oneself, to become conscious and master of oneself so that one never sets a bad example to one's child.

For it is above all through example that education becomes effective. To speak good words and to give wise advice to a child has very little effect if one does not oneself give him an example of what one teaches. Sincerity, honesty, straightforwardness, courage, disinterestedness, unselfishness, patience, endurance, perseverance, peace, calm, self-control are all things that are taught infinitely better by example than by beautiful speeches.

Parents, have a high ideal and always act in accordance with it and you will see that little by little your child will reflect this ideal in himself and spontaneously manifest the qualities you would like to see expressed in his nature. Quite naturally a child has respect and admiration for his parents; unless they are quite unworthy, they will always appear to their child as demigods whom he will try to imitate as best he can.

With very few exceptions, parents are not aware of the disastrous influence that their own defects, impulses, weaknesses and lack of self-control have on their children. If you wish to be respected by a child, have respect for yourself and be worthy of respect at every moment. Never be authoritarian, despotic, impatient or ill-tempered. When your child asks you a question, do not give him a stupid or silly answer under the pretext that he cannot understand you. You can always make yourself understood if you take enough trouble; and in spite of the popular saying that it is not always good to tell the truth, I affirm that it is always good to tell the truth, but that the art consists in telling it in such a way as to make it accessible to the mind of the hearer.

In early life, until he is twelve or fourteen, the child's mind is hardly open to abstract notions and general ideas. And yet you can train it to understand these things by using concrete images, symbols or parables. Up to quite an advanced age and for some who mentally always remain children, a narrative, a story, a tale well told teach much more than any number of theoretical explanations.

Another pitfall to avoid: do not scold your child without good reason and only when it is quite indispensable. A child who is too often scolded gets hardened to rebuke and no longer attaches much importance to words or severity of tone. And above all, take good care never to scold him for a fault which you yourself commit. Children are very keen and clear-sighted observers; they soon find out your weaknesses and note them without pity.

When a child has done something wrong, see that he confesses it to you spontaneously and frankly; and when he has confessed, with kindness and affection make him understand what was wrong in his movement so that he will not repeat it, but never scold him; a fault confessed must always be forgiven. You should not allow any fear to come between you and your child; fear is a pernicious means of education: it invariably gives birth to deceit and lying. Only a discerning affection that is firm yet gentle and an adequate practical knowledge will create the bonds of trust that are indispensable for you to be able to educate your child effectively. And do not forget that you have to control yourself constantly in order to be equal to your task and truly fulfil the duty which you owe your child by the mere fact of having brought him into the world.

NEP 2020 policy was a paradigm shift, it took time to be well understood, implemented and the results were not visible before 2030. Those were the formative years challenging the almost 200 years old Education system having its foundations in the Indian Education Act 1835. Post 2030 the policy implementation started bearing fruit, as I clearly see today in 2050.

Some examples of Paradigm shifts. In schools across the curriculum from grades 1 through 12, the subjects of Sanskrit, yoga, and meditation were integrated into the educational framework. Far from being perceived solely as a religious language, Sanskrit was revered as the linguistic foundation from which many Indian languages had evolved. Its ancient texts were esteemed repositories of profound wisdom, offering insights into the attainment of human completeness, self-realization, and spiritual enlightenment. The belief persisted that the knowledge encapsulated within Sanskrit had the transformative potential to rejuvenate the cultural heritage, or Sanskriti, that seemed to have waned over time. This reservoir of wisdom was deemed capable of rejuvenating the dwindling Sanskriti, or cultural ethos, of the nation.

Concurrently, yoga and meditation had transcended cultural boundaries to become universally embraced practices cherished for their ability to facilitate a fulfilling and balanced life. Their inclusion in the school curriculum played a pivotal role not only at physical well-being but also at fostering mental clarity and emotional resilience among students. By embracing these age-old disciplines, Indian schools sought to instill in students a holistic approach to personal development, equipping them with the tools to navigate life with purpose and resilience.

The restructuring of the syllabus and rewriting of textbooks represented a concerted effort to embed India's rich historical legacy into the educational framework. Each subject was presented through the lens of India's contributions, allowing young learners to trace the evolution of human knowledge and civilization. The syllabi underwent a comprehensive overhaul, with textbooks meticulously revised to incorporate the historical contributions of India across various subjects. Children were no longer taught vested interests coated in facts like this one - *"Till a few hundred years back, humans thought that the earth was flat and we could fall, if we walked to its edge."*

By elucidating the evolution of each discipline, including India's contribution, i.e. teaching all subjects, all topics in totality helped them connect the dots, build the flow, and develop respect for ancient and modern India's contribution to the subjects. All school subjects taught the evolution of the subjects or topics, starting from the findings of the ancient past (of India) and connecting to the modern discoveries and developments. Educators thus instilled in young learners a deep appreciation for the profound legacy of ancient Indian knowledge and innovation.

Moreover, a novel pedagogical approach was adopted, emphasizing the interconnectedness of all subjects. By studying diverse fields holistically, students were encouraged to discern patterns, forge connections, and cultivate a coherent understanding of the world. This interdisciplinary approach not only fostered intellectual curiosity but also fostered a profound respect for the enduring contributions of ancient Indian civilization. Students while graduating from high school or senior secondary schools were more prepared for higher studies or research.

In addition to these curricular changes, students' school diaries and almanacs which served as repositories of wisdom, were adorned with an eclectic mix of sayings and proverbs sourced from both Western and Indian traditions. This deliberate juxtaposition aimed to broaden students' perspectives, nurturing a sense of cultural pluralism while fostering a deep-seated pride in the rich heritage of ancient India.

Collectively, these initiatives transcend traditional paradigms of education, fostering a generation of learners equipped not only with academic knowledge but also with the wisdom and insight necessary to navigate life's complexities with purpose and resilience.

Recognizing the strain caused by heavy school bags, educational authorities undertook a significant overhaul of the daily timetable. Students' schedules were revamped to include a more manageable load, with a reduced number of classes (periods) ranging from 3 to 6 per day aligning with the grade level and complexity of the subject matter. Each class (period) was extended to a duration of one hour. This restructuring aimed to address the inadequacies of shorter class periods lasting only 30 to 40 minutes, which were deemed insufficient for comprehensive learning. Many boards have adopted no homework as a policy.

Drawing inspiration from time-tested educational practices rooted in ancient Indian wisdom, educators embraced the concept of teaching fewer subjects each day, ideally distributed throughout the week. This strategic adjustment sought to foster deeper comprehension and create space for experiential learning opportunities. With more time allocated to each subject, students got the opportunity for in-depth exploration and immersion in the material. This immersive approach enabled students to engage more meaningfully with the content, leading to a heightened understanding and appreciation of the topics covered.

The benefits of this shift extended beyond the physical realm, as it also alleviated the cognitive burden on students. By providing ample time for reflection, discussion, and practical application of concepts, the new schedule promoted a more balanced and effective learning experience. Students were encouraged to delve deeper into their studies, cultivating critical thinking skills and a genuine passion for learning. Ultimately, the restructuring of the timetable represented a holistic approach to education, prioritizing the well-being and academic success of students.

Additionally, to achieve quality education in rural areas, following measures were taken. Execution of the ambitious plan to ensure that all six lakh villages across India to be equipped with high-quality higher secondary or vocational schools having proficient teachers. Additionally, it was implemented that each of these rural educational institutions would host adult education programs throughout various hours of the day. This initiative mirrored a return to ancient practices, where temples served as bustling community hubs, fostering education, political discourse, and cultural exchanges.

In line with this historical precedent, the schools under village panchayats' jurisdiction were slated for expansion to fulfil a similar role as modern-day community centers by the establishment of Common Service Centers (CSC) or *suvidha kendras* within these educational facilities. This strategic move transformed schools into vibrant hubs for villages or panchayats, offering not only educational services but also essential government and business services directly to citizens' doorsteps. A significant budget allocation was earmarked for the establishment of 100,000 CSCs in rural areas and 10,000 in urban

India, indicative of the administration's commitment to grassroots development.

The partnership between schools and CSCs held the promise of numerous benefits for villages and panchayats. This collaboration optimized resource utilization, curtailed unnecessary infrastructure expenses, and transformed schools-CSCs into pivotal centers for disseminating government initiatives and addressing citizens' grievances effectively. These plans were realized, they proved a bold vision for holistic community development and citizen empowerment.

The century old problem of absence of true moral education in schools and colleges posed a significant threat to societal values. Towards the end of the 20th century, moral education had progressively dwindled, reduced to a mere subject known as moral science in some schools, while being entirely absent in others. This decline was attributed to the rise of newer, more enticing subjects that catered to economic interests. As a result, a concerning trend emerged wherein respect for teachers and elders sharply declined. This phenomenon was linked to the diminishing quality of educators, stemming from the rapid proliferation of educational institutions and intense competition, resulting in the appointment of subpar teachers. However, culpability also lay with parents who, instead of offering constructive feedback privately to teachers, resorted to criticizing them in front of students, leading to the erosion of respect.

Addressing the deficiency in moral education required concerted efforts from both educational institutions and parents, schools prioritized the reinstatement of moral education in their curriculum, integrating it seamlessly into various subjects to ensure holistic development. Simultaneously, parents fostered an environment conducive to respectful discourse and constructive feedback, nurturing a culture of mutual understanding and collaboration between educators and guardians.

Ancient Indian anecdotes and stories became an integral part of formal teaching. Ultimately, reinstating moral education and fostering mutual respect between teachers, parents, and students was essential for nurturing responsible, ethical citizens capable of navigating the complexities of the modern world with integrity and compassion.

Major steps were taken for the adult (re) education as well. The vision was clear: every adult in India was to receive comprehensive education in the complete history of the nation, thereby ensuring that the mistakes of our ancestors were not repeated. It was imperative for people to grasp the profound contributions made by our forebears across all domains and disciplines.

Moreover, there was a concerted effort to encourage every working professional to engage in enrichment courses tailored to their respective fields, whether literature, art, construction, science, engineering, medicine, or beyond. These courses were designed not only to impart knowledge but also to trace the evolutionary journey of each subject, from ancient wisdom to contemporary advancements.

The implementation of such enrichment courses offered flexibility, with options for online learning or attendance at evening or weekend schools. Governments, schools, along with their partners, were poised to leverage various communication channels, including TV, radio, and Internet/OTT platforms, to disseminate this knowledge widely and effectively. This strategic utilization of media aimed to reach individuals across diverse demographics and geographical locations, ensuring equitable access to educational resources. Largely it happened.

Crucially, local communities were empowered to take proactive steps in fostering a culture of continuous learning and knowledge sharing. Rather than waiting for government initiatives, communities were encouraged to initiate peer learning groups, thereby creating grassroots networks of mutual support and intellectual exchange. This bottom-up approach not only complemented top-down efforts but also empowered individuals to take ownership of their learning journey.

The envisioned outcome was a society where every citizen was equipped with a deep understanding of their cultural heritage and professional field. By bridging the gap between past and present, these initiatives continuously instill a sense of pride in our shared history and inspire innovation and excellence in various domains. Through continuous learning and collaborative efforts, individuals contribute meaningfully to the advancement and prosperity of the nation, building a brighter future for generations to come.

6 Governance System Overhaul

Today is 14th April 2050. India celebrates this as Dr. B.R. Ambedkar jayanti. Dr. Ambedkar's contributions have had a profound and lasting impact on Indian society, shaping its democratic institutions, promoting social justice, and empowering marginalized communities. He remains an iconic figure in India's struggle for equality and justice. He is revered as the architect of the Indian Constitution, advocate for social justice, leader of the dalit movement, etc.

In 1947, India was declared independent in a haste. After gaining independence, India continued to follow the British style (Westminster system) of Governance structure, having Legislature (Parliamentary system), Legal structure and Laws (Judicial system), Administrative and Taxation (Executive system), and ICS became IAS. Military structure, Police structure and more importantly the attitudes remained very

British. The British adopted system of governance, justice and administration had made the Indian judges, the political leaders and the administrative officers out of reach of the common Indian man. The common man was already devastated by the violence of partition that came with independence and was being further alienated. Even after 70-80 years of gaining independence, they remained unreachable for the common people, except during the times of elections or protests. Selfish political parties ensured that society remains divided along the line of classes, castes, region, language, color and religion. These parties fanned such divisions in the general elections of 2019, 2024, and even in 2029. Not a healthy sign.

21st century India was craving for democratic reforms. "Of the People, By the People, For the People" was not working, actually. The democratic ecosystem of the last century was not sufficient to lead the country in the 21st century. We had seen in the past that not the best people come into active politics. MPs, MLAs, Parshads, etc many a times were criminal turned politicians, many were nearly illiterates, many non sincere about the usage of powers or position, many corrupt to core, and many anti-nationals having other interests. Very few among them were God fearing, people caring, selfless people with good intentions. I recall that in the year 2020-21, out of the 4 crores cases pending across the courts of India, 4 lakhs were on the people active in politics.

In administration, people who aspired to give service to the nation worked hard, studied hard to become trained administrators (bureaucrats or babus). However, many times they worked under the orders of the non competent politicians holding the positions of decisions.

Celebrated Field Marshal Sam Manekshaw had once remarked on the incompetence of the ministers and secretaries of his times. According to him, and several other true leaders, a political person holding power should be competent enough to understand the issues, participate in the debates and take decisions, especially when the country's name, progress, security and existence is at stake! Incompetent ministers who don't understand the gravity of the situation and consequences of the hastily taken decisions', will often say like one said to the Field Marshal when India was planning attack on erstwhile east Pakistan "Maan jao na Shaam - meaning Please agree to it Sam"!

By the time we saw 2029 general elections, significant changes were brought into the political system, some are listed as follows:

- Ruling party was called the "Serving" party. The word "serving" held a powerful message, it is keeping the much needed check on the "ways of thinking and ways of working" of the people in power. "Serving" reminds them that they are temporary electives of the people, and they have themselves chosen the path to serve the people and nation. This small but significant shift has brought sincerity, mindfulness and compassion in politicians' thoughts, speech and work.

- Opposition party was called the "Supporting" party. The compelling difference between the words "opposition and supporting" is well understood. It reminds the party not in power that you are here to support; people of India want you to support the government and help them make true progress. It nudges them that you are elected by the people not to blindly oppose but to align on the important matters, keeping the national interests at top priority. It reminds them that you are not sent here to walk out or run away from your responsibilities!

- "Vote out" option was brought into action. A robust feedback system was implemented by the government, in which each voter (citizen) could anytime participate through the phone call, through the website, or through the mobile application or other means of communication to cast "vote out". A voter could choose the option to vote out the elected person of his/her constituency, if the voter considers the elected person is not performing well. This established a mechanism which empowered the citizens to actively participate in the development of their constituency. No more agitations, or dharna were observed after 2030. This change, which was introduced during the 2024-2029 term, brought accountability among the chosen ones (i.e., the elected ones). Initially the vote out mechanism was implemented at the ward level i.e. at the municipality (city) level, and the panchayat level. After due diligence of making it robust and flawless, and transparent, it was implemented for state legislature and parliament as well.

- The law that provided for lifelong pensions for Members of Parliament (MPs) and Members of Legislative Assemblies (MLAs) is the "Pension Act of 1954". This act entitled former MPs and MLAs to receive a pension for their service life long. This was challenged, debated, and finally quashed as it was found to be irrelevant and an overhead.

- There were no specific educational qualifications required by law for the candidates contesting elections for central or state levels. They often had varying levels of education, many have been nearly illiterates and incompetent. The bar was raised, minimum qualification became post graduation, with demonstrated social / cultural

/ economic accomplishments, and clear vision for the country (what needs to be done, why, how and by when?), etc. Thus the cleanup was done. Incompetent and selfish were thrown out.

- In the year 2025, the Indian government had adopted 2047 as the single toll-free phone number to help citizens participate in the governance, give feedback on schemes, including "vote out" mechanism. This number also served as a reminder to all to achieve the developed nation goal of 2047. Today in 2050, telephonic support for all Government to Citizen (G2C) services have moved to this number. This service is powered by Artificial Intelligence, for having voice communication in all the dialects spoken in our country. Even the users not using smartphones, like super senior citizens or poor people or even small children, get the same experience when they call.

By design, Indian systems of governance had the three pillars in legislative, executive (administrative) and judiciary systems. The Legislature had direct interference in the administration, which had prevented the country from making true progress.

For example: By design of the Indian constitution, law and order was the state subject. The state level politicians had direct control over the state's police. They continued to use the police as their puppets. By their control of police, harassment of senior police officials and threats of transfers to remote places, etc. local politicians caused lawlessness in their constituencies and hence to the state and country. After the year 2025, many senior police officials told frustrating stories of how they were forced to do corrupt things over decades, under the pressure of the state politicians. That was the tip of the iceberg. That triggered constitutional debates of making the law and order, as a central subject, i.e. to make police in control of the central government like paramilitary and military forces. Below were some of the benefits for this move:

- Central government can tackle law and order for the country holistically, without state governments' hindrance.

- Central intelligence, armed forces, para-military and police working in tandem can minimize loop-holes and tackle terrorism in a better way.

- Like armed forces and central paramilitary forces, corruption in the police force will decline significantly. The police force can again become fit, efficient and accountable helping them earn the lost trust and respect from the masses.

- Local and state politicians will automatically become aware of their responsibilities, will not manoeuvre police and corruption will reduce significantly.

- State government departments, especially the public dealing departments, will function better. The officials there will have to realize that state politicians don't control the police anymore.

- Police can work without fear of transfers, suspensions and bullying by the local politicians.

- There will be more transparency. FIRs will be lodged without fear from local politicians.

In the year 2030, law and order became the central subject. Since the last 20 years, India has seen a steep rise in adherence to law. I recall during my younger days I aspired to become a country like Singapore. In terms of law and order, we have become that!

Unthinkable happened in the year 2047. A new system of self-governance is under formation. Based upon the feedback received on the citizen portals - including the G2C toll-free number 2047, and via surveys, research, contemplation and debates, and with guidance from spiritual people, India is reforming its 100+ years old Governance structure which was given by the British raj. Soon, the parliamentary system of governance will be replaced by the Presidential - Governors - PPP (Executive) administration system.

PPP model as we know means Public Private Partnership model. PPP model was tried successfully in infrastructure development projects, during the years 2011-2030. Later it was tested on the new mega towns' planning, new state capitals' planning, old towns' replanning, rural areas replanning, industry redevelopment and relocation, agro-production and associated supply-chains, vocational skills development for local industry and prevention of mass migrations, inclusion of 100% citizens in government direct benefits schemes, taxations, energy and multi-modal transportation, alleviation of poverty, holistic health and education for all, etc. All these participations encompass development and care for the human resources and cautious utilization of the natural resources. In nutshell that is what governments are meant for.

A new class of (executive) administrative service is being developed, taking inspiration from the successful 100+ years of the armed forces' training process. Idea is to produce more competent executives. Every state now has specialised higher education institutes of eminence for the "to-be" servants (administrators). Unlike the IAS/IFS/IPS/etc training of 1-2 years, these "to-be" servants after completing their schooling will have 4-6 years of rigorous training rooted in Indian values blended with modern outlook. These institutes will produce the best in class individuals with a nation first attitude, who will have selfless serving attitude, compassion for all, desire for true service for the people, aspiration to serve their motherland and competence and wisdom to work in their areas of choice.

During their training they will apprentice in the PPP administration to develop interests and learn the functioning. Until anyones specially asks for it, upon completion of their training they will become part of the PPP administration of their home state. By the time they join the PPP administration, they will be equipped to work with minimal guidance, and take right decisions. They will be responsible for the progress, accountable for the failures, and will be sacked by the people if they get significant negative feedback from the citizens' portals and from the toll-free 2047. They will rise to become the Governors, and eventually President of India. Thus the governance structure will become transparent, competent, accountable and modern, which is needed for the 21st century.

In the pilot Nation-first districts, PPP will replace the rural and urban local governments, then expand to take over states, and ultimately central governance.

Soon, the electoral process will give way to the Presidential - Governors - PPP (Executive) administration structure for transparent governance, where citizens will have power to evaluate and sack the low performers. That's the true democracy.

7 Socio-Economic, Cultural renaissance

भूखे पेट भजन नहीं होय (an empty stomach can't sing praise of God) is an old saying in India. This is quite true.

Dr. APJ Abdul Kalam in his book "Ignited Minds" asserts that "Not any country, but poverty is the biggest enemy of India and it is preventing India from unlocking its true potential". In their 200 years of subjugation, the British had brought down India from being the richest in the world to one of the poorest countries. Millions of untimely deaths, due to enforced poverty and planned famines, are attributed to the British period. Britain recently apologised for it, India having a big heart pardoned Britain!

Alleviation of Poverty

The Indian government recognised "poverty is the biggest enemy" and worked towards it. Governments focussed on the fundamental needs of any family, and made true efforts to provide those supplies and services to them, for years. That helped them stand on their feet, by ensuring that they don't have to worry about where will they live, what will they eat, how will they cook, where will their children study, how will they pay for treatment of their ailments, where will they get training for vocational skills, from where will they get interest free micro loans, how to avail subsidies on staple food, electricity, tools & farm equipments, how to avail insurances in times of need, etc.

Assurance for availability of above mentioned basic needs was necessary for relieving pressure of living, for a poor family. These needs were taken care of by the governments, without any financial burden to the hundreds of millions of people, for over two decades 2015-2035. Now the efforts are bearing fruit, as there is no family in India which is poor or dependent on others for help. Each family in India is financially independent. India has achieved true Independence in 2050.

Below are just a few examples, many other social and economic welfare schemes executed in India for addressing needs and challenges across different sections of society.

Pradhan Mantri Jan Dhan Yojana (PMJDY): By opening zero balance accounts for hundreds of millions of poor, this scheme formed the bedrock for digital financial inclusion. It provided access to various financial services like savings accounts, Direct benefits transfers for above mentioned schemes, insurance, and pension to the unbanked population. This eliminated the role of middlemen.

Pradhan Mantri Suraksha Bima Yojana (PMSBY): PMSBY was an accidental insurance scheme that provided coverage for accidental death and disability at a nominal premium. Many rural individuals, including farmers, were beneficiaries of this scheme. This gave them moral support, that someone is here for them.

Pradhan Mantri Jeevan Jyoti Bima Yojana (PMJJBY): Similar to PMSBY, PMJJBY was a life insurance scheme providing coverage for death due to any reason. It offered financial security to the beneficiaries, including farmers, at a low premium.

Pradhan Mantri Ujjwala Yojana (PMUY): PMUY provided clean cooking fuel in the form of LPG (liquefied petroleum gas) to millions of poor households. The scheme reduced health hazards associated with traditional cooking fuels like wood and cow dung. Benefits include improved health outcomes for women, time-saving, and environmental benefits.

Pradhan Mantri Awas Yojana (PMAY): PMAY provided affordable housing to all eligible beneficiaries, urban and rural poor who never had their own homes. The scheme addressed the housing needs of the economically weaker sections and low-income groups. Benefits include access to safe and affordable housing, improved living conditions, and infrastructure development.

National Rural Livelihoods Mission (NRLM): NRLM alleviated rural poverty by promoting self-employment and entrepreneurship through various livelihood initiatives. The scheme focused on organizing rural poor into self-help groups and provided them with financial assistance, skills development, and market linkages. Benefits include income generation, skills development, and women empowerment.

Ayushman Bharat Pradhan Mantri Jan Arogya Yojana (PM-JAY): PM-JAY was the world's largest health insurance scheme that provided cashless coverage to over 100 million vulnerable families. The scheme reduced out-of-pocket healthcare expenses and provided financial protection to the poor families, against health expenditures.

Swachh Bharat Abhiyan (Clean India Mission): This scheme achieved universal sanitation and cleanliness by constructing toilets, eliminating open defecation, and managing solid waste. Improved public health, reduction in waterborne diseases, enhanced dignity and safety, and environmental sustainability. It was started on 2nd October 2014.

Sarva Shiksha Abhiyan (SSA): SSA provided universal access to quality elementary education for all children in the 6-14 age group. The scheme improved infrastructure, teacher recruitment and training, and the retention of students. Benefits include increased literacy rates, improved educational outcomes, and reduced dropout rates.

Much of India still stays in villages. Major initiatives were taken to address various aspects of rural life, including infrastructure, healthcare, education, agriculture, entrepreneurship and employment generation. These focussed areas reflect the government's commitment to holistic rural development and improving the quality of life in villages across India.

Rural Infrastructure Development: The government focused on improving basic infrastructure such as roads, electricity, water supply, sanitation, and housing in rural areas to enhance living standards and facilitate economic activities.

Agriculture and Rural Economy: Initiatives like the Pradhan Mantri Krishi Sinchayee Yojana (PMKSY) improved irrigation facilities, promoted sustainable agricultural practices, provided credit facilities, and enhanced market linkages for farmers.

Rural Employment Generation: Schemes like the Mahatma Gandhi National Rural Employment Guarantee Act (MGNREGA) provided employment opportunities to rural households by guaranteeing fixed number of days of wage employment in a financial year. Lots of rural infrastructure development happened from this fund. Every village developed at least a new large pond which helped in ground water recharging.

Rural Health and Sanitation: The government focused on improving healthcare facilities in rural areas through initiatives such as the National Rural Health Mission (NRHM) and the Swachh Bharat Abhiyan, provided access to healthcare services and promoted sanitation and hygiene practices.

Rural Education: Rigorous efforts were made to improve access to quality education in rural areas through initiatives like the Sarva Shiksha Abhiyan (SSA) and the Rashtriya Madhyamik Shiksha Abhiyan (RMSA), which ensured universal elementary and secondary education under the NEP 2020 guidelines.

Rural Connectivity: The government improved connectivity in rural areas through initiatives like the BharatNet project, which provided broadband connectivity to all villages, and the Pradhan Mantri

Gram Sadak Yojana (PMGSY), which connected rural areas with all-weather roads.

Rural Development and Governance: Various schemes and programs were implemented to strengthen rural governance, promote local self-governance institutions such as Panchayati Raj Institutions (PRIs), and empowered rural communities to participate in decision-making processes.

Pradhan Mantri Fasal Bima Yojana (PMFBY): This scheme provided insurance coverage and financial support to farmers in the event of crop failure due to natural calamities, pests, and diseases. It ensured comprehensive risk coverage, and the premium rates were subsidized by the central and state governments.

Weather-Based Crop Insurance Scheme (WBCIS): WBCIS was designed to provide protection to farmers against adverse weather conditions that lead to crop losses. It used weather parameters to assess crop losses.

The Indian government actively promoted village tourism as part of its broader efforts to boost rural development and tourism. Some initiatives and efforts undertaken by the Indian government to promote village tourism as listed below:

Swadesh Darshan Scheme: The Ministry of Tourism launched the Swadesh Darshan Scheme to develop thematic circuits in the country, one of which focused on rural and village tourism. Under this scheme, funds were allocated for the development of tourism infrastructure, amenities, and services in rural areas to attract tourists. Today we have more than 100 thematic tourist circuits flourishing in India, where each circuit takes 1-2 weeks to explore. If anyone wants to explore India, he/she would need at least two years!

Community-Based Tourism Initiatives: Various state governments in India launched community-based tourism initiatives wherein local communities got actively involved in tourism activities. These initiatives focussed on promoting rural experiences, traditional crafts, local cuisine, and cultural heritage. Millions of rural homestays are running as a part of this scheme.

Training and Capacity Building: The government conducted training programs and capacity-building workshops for rural communities to equip them with the necessary skills and knowledge to engage with tourists effectively. These efforts empowered locals to participate in and benefit from tourism activities.

Marketing and Promotion: The Ministry of Tourism, as well as state tourism boards, actively promoted village tourism through marketing campaigns, roadshows, and participation in travel fairs and exhibitions both domestically and internationally.

Infrastructure Development: The government invested heavily in improving infrastructure in rural areas, including roads, electricity, sanitation facilities, and accommodation options, to enhance the overall tourism experience for visitors.

Adopt a Heritage Scheme: While not solely focused on village tourism, this scheme encouraged public sector companies, private sector companies, and individuals to adopt heritage sites, including those in rural areas, for development and maintenance.

After achieving the 100% digitization of land records, the initiative to promote community farming within villages was actively pursued from the year 2030. Farmers were encouraged to unite all farms and fields, fostering a sense of collective responsibility towards agricultural practices. Existing land sharing policies underwent thorough scrutiny and adjustments to ensure they were more accommodating and supportive. Empowering the farmers, they were entrusted with the collective decision-making process regarding what crops to cultivate in the vast fields, while individual ownership rights remained intact.

The consolidation of land into larger fields stimulated innovation and boosted agricultural productivity, yielding a higher produce per acre. This structural adjustment mitigated the financial strain on families during times of crop failure, potentially alleviating the burden of debts and curbing instances of farmer suicides significantly. Moreover, the consolidation mitigated personal rivalries that often stemmed from the division of fields.

Furthermore, facilitating the sharing of machinery among farmers was observed as a strategic move to optimize resource utilization and foster rural entrepreneurship. By encouraging collaboration and mutual support, the initiative could create a more sustainable and prosperous agricultural community, benefiting both individual farmers and the village as a whole.

Here it is important to note that India's entrepreneurial landscape has undergone a significant transformation over the past few decades, propelled by a dynamic blend of factors ranging from economic reforms to technological advancements and cultural shifts. The culture of entrepreneurship in India is characterized by resilience, innovation, and a flourishing spirit of risk-taking.

One of the key drivers behind India's entrepreneurial surge is its large and youthful population, which provides a fertile ground for fresh ideas and ventures. Additionally, the country's rapidly expanding middle and high income class, coupled with internet penetration, created a vast consumer market ripe for innovation and disruption.

Cultural factors also contributed significantly to India's entrepreneurial ethos. Historically, entrepreneurship has been ingrained in the Indian psyche, since the times of silk-route. With a long tradition of family-owned businesses and small-scale enterprises, this entrepreneurial spirit was revitalized by a new generation of innovators leveraging technology to solve pressing societal challenges and create impact-driven businesses.

Economic renaissance

Economics is fundamentally utilization of natural resources, and making the best use of people's skills and abilities. But sometimes, it is hard to tell when we are using things wisely or taking advantage of them too much. This can cause big problems that we might not notice right away, even though we think we are making progress. In the last century, the way we thought about getting ahead mostly focused on growing the economy really fast, without thinking much about what might happen later on. This led to a bunch of problems like pollution and unfairness (economic divide). If we had not paid more attention to how we use natural resources and treat people, these problems would have gotten worse. So, it was super important for us to figure out how to use things in a smart and fair way, and to make sure everyone can thrive without harming the planet.

After becoming the third largest world economy, India needed to see that in the race for higher GDP, it did not over consume its finite natural resources. Else, it would have been left with no choice but to import those resources from other countries. In fact, India realised that it should come out of the blind race of markets & GDP growth. It realised it should see what was truly required for its people to lead a respectable and holistic life, by critically analyzing what was available in our country and what was missing but truly needed.

That's what India retrospected in the year 2030, what was good for its future. It was clear that it should protect its finite natural resources, keep control on mining and deforestation being done in the name of exports and growth. There should be at least a 100 year view with respect to all natural resources.

Ministries dealing with natural resources needed to have assessed the profit and losses of the long-term view. Why were certain mining activities considered absolutely necessary? Why were certain new dams absolutely necessary? Reverse the natural resources disasters we had created in the past 50 years, or else mother nature would do it in the next 25 years. A thorough assessment was done by all ministries/departments, for gains and losses of the last 50 years. Plans were made to compensate for all past losses in the next 10 years.

Concerned ministries have done a critical assessment of exports – How were the foreign countries using the raw materials from India? Why do they need those raw materials from India; were they hiding or saving their reserves? Which products did they make from those raw materials? Did they re-export those products back to India; i.e. did India import those finished products? Did we really need those products, or was it due to lobbying by corrupt Indians and the marketing industry which created fake markets? What loss was India making in exporting those raw materials (depletion of natural resources and pollution)? Immediate banning of all exports which harmed India's interests and depleted natural resources, was done.

Concerned ministries did a critical assessment of imports as well – What was being imported? Why was it needed in India? How could it be produced here? They aimed for local production and zero imports in 10 years, and made it happen.

A 100 year plan was made with the consent of all the major political parties, the think tanks, and a fair representation of spiritual people who understood the importance of the 5 basic elements which formed life and nature (air, water, earth, fire, and akash/space). This 100 year plan became the guidelines for our country to move forward in the right direction. India became Independent in true economic sense by the year 2047.

Cultural renaissance

India has long been celebrated for its open and welcoming culture, a tradition that spans centuries. Central to this ethos is the profound value placed on questioning. Unlike mere adherence to instructions or directives, Indian culture encourages deep inquiry and exploration. This ethos has given rise to a multitude of schools of thought, each emerging from diverse paths of realization. Despite their differences, these various philosophies invariably converge upon a singular truth: the absolute.

Through centuries of philosophical discourse and spiritual introspection, India has fostered an environment where individuals are free to explore the depths of their understanding and seek truth in its purest form. This rich tapestry of thought has woven its way into the very fabric of Indian society, shaping its traditions, beliefs, and way of life. From the ancient Vedas to the teachings of modern-day gurus, the spirit of inquiry continues to thrive, affirming India's enduring legacy as a beacon of intellectual curiosity and spiritual enlightenment.

Indian philosophy emphasizes inner growth over external expansion, urging individuals to delve deep into their own selves rather than seeking outward conquests. It advocates a profound introspection, encouraging individuals to explore the infinite depths of their consciousness. This approach stands in stark contrast to ideologies that discourage critical inquiry and blind adherence to authority, which have historically resulted in the suppression and oppression of diverse cultures. India's rich history bears witness to such challenges endured over millennia. By prioritizing internal evolution, Indian thought fosters personal development and spiritual enlightenment, offering a pathway to harmony and understanding in an interconnected world.

Throughout history, India has served as a sanctuary for oppressed civilizations, including Jews and Persians (original Iranians), who found refuge and made it their home. Christian saints and Islamic sufis journeyed to India, embracing its diverse culture as their own. The indigenous population warmly welcomed them, fostering a harmonious blending akin to sugar dissolving in milk. This rich tapestry of acceptance and integration showcases India's legacy as a melting pot of cultures, where differences are celebrated and embraced, contributing to the vibrant mosaic of Indian society.

This narrative of tolerance and understanding reverberated throughout various spheres of society, permeating educational institutions, social gatherings, spiritual assemblies, and cultural events. Within the intimate settings of religious venues, households, and workplaces, this message found fertile ground for growth and acceptance. Over time, the divisive barriers erected by differences in worship, language, region, religion, color, caste, or creed gradually dissolved.

In this evolution, religious leaders emerged as catalysts for change, assuming pivotal roles in guiding governments, courts, and communities towards a more inclusive and harmonious ethos. Their efforts aimed to dispel the notion that any faith's teachings should sow seeds of alienation, exclusion, or animosity towards others. Instead, they underscored the fundamental unity of humanity, emphasizing the mutual respect and significance inherent in all belief systems.

Drawing upon the analogy of fingers forming a fist, they advocated for the coexistence of diverse belief systems, stressing the importance of preserving individual privacy, faith, and possessions. Through collaboration and understanding, they envisioned a path towards genuine progress, where the richness of diversity could flourish without fear or prejudice, fostering a society bound by empathy, respect, and mutual appreciation.

Everyone acknowledged the necessity of unwavering faith in the country's constitution, prioritizing national interests, respecting diverse lifestyles, and safeguarding each other's privacy and beliefs. This collective commitment fostered unity and mutual understanding, laying the foundation for a harmonious and inclusive society. This paved the way for Socio-Cultural renaissance in India.

8 A transformed India

I am back on my bench today. It is 15th August 2050 and I am summarising the factors that brought the transformations in the life of people of my country.

Inner transformations

Indian thought is traditionally anchored on some fundamental realisations. When there was no other religion in the world, Indian saints had developed the dharmic way of leading life of a purpose. Purpose was to know the Supreme; reach to Him. Self discovery is said to be the first step towards that goal. In this process do good to others, thereby assimilating good karma (deeds). This process has fundamental guiding principles, which everyone living in the country should understand, irrespective of their faith. This would help to align with the Indic roots, and it does not mean to get influenced with the Indian originating religions.

Judaism, Christianity, and Islam initially flourished in the Jerusalem or Arabian region, before they spread to the other parts of the world. It is but natural, that Indians who are devoted to these faiths may not have been told about the Indigenous beliefs and principles. This may have caused some alienation in the previous centuries.

During the last 20 years, every child and adult was taught the fundamental teachings of all religions practised freely in India. They were taught by religious leaders or teachers. They were encouraged to enquire, and learn more about any religion or faith. Even the atheists participated. This practice resulted in the development of understanding new perspectives of life, religious tolerance i.e. respect for others' faith or religion.

Living in India requires that people know the traditional Indian thought which is anchored on the principle of inclusion. Some of those principles are explained briefly below:

अहं ब्रह्मास्मि - *I am Brahm* (the Supreme soul), meaning "I am that divine force within". This means that all humans are alike.

वसुधैव कुटुंबकम् - *Vasudhaiva Kutumbakam*, meaning "the whole world is a family". This means all living beings are my family.

सर्वे भवन्तु सुखिनः सर्वे सन्तु निरामयाः । सर्वे भद्राणि पश्यन्तु मा कश्चिद्दुःखभाग्भवेत् । ॐ शान्तिः शान्तिः शान्तिः ॥ *Sarve Bhavantu Sukhinah Sarve Santu Niramayaah. Sarve Bhadrani Pashyantu Ma Kashchidduhkhabhagbhavet.* Om shantih shantih shantih, meaning "May all be happy, may all be disease-free, may all be witnesses of auspicious events and may no one have to suffer sorrow". This simply means may all live happily.

कण कण में भगवान - *God is omnipresent*. This is self explanatory.

Above four principles make the foundation of original Indic thought. These are inclusive and caring at the core.

Sri Aurobindo wrote extensively about Indic wisdom. He gave the three fold principle of self discovery, self development and fulfilment; those are Swabhava, Swadhyay, and Swadharma. Swabhava refers to one's inherent nature or disposition, shaped by genetics, upbringing, and experiences. Swadhyay is the practice of self-study, reflecting on one's thoughts, actions, and beliefs to gain self-awareness and personal growth. Swadharma is one's unique duty or purpose in life, aligned with their innate qualities and values. Understanding Swabhava helps individuals identify their Swadharma, while Swadhyay facilitates introspection to live in accordance with it. Embracing Swadharma leads to fulfilment and harmony, as individuals authentically engage with their roles and responsibilities, contributing positively to themselves and society. This approach was universally accepted as the way to lead a purposeful life, and was taught at schools.

People also learnt to differentiate between need and greed, growth and prosperity, achievements and fulfilment, and most importantly overcoming fears, as it is often seen that our life is driven or shaped by fears. These realisations were possible once people read and followed the great people of the past, when they chose an apt role model for their life who had immensely contributed to the society and nation.

Nation's transformations

There were a number of turning points in recent history, which made India, a prosperous, peaceful, responsible, and Vishwamitra (friend of all) country. Some of the prominent ones are construction of Shri Ram mandir and Muhammad bin Abdullah masjid at Ayodhya, Shri Ram being hailed as Rashtra-Pita (Father of the Nation) in the year 2047 (Gandhi ji's soul would have been the happiest on this day, as he was a devotee of Prabhu Shri Ram), Establishment of the fact that Jesus Christ lived in Kashmir, Mahaavtar baba ji and Jesus are same soul, cultural reunion of Indian subcontinent, Kashmir being instrumental to resolve the Jews/Muslims conflict and in kindling east/west spiritual reunion, geo-political corrections in China and Tibet, commencement of Bharat Maharatna, general acceptance that Netaji Subhas Chandra Bose lived in Ayodhya till he left for heavenly abode in the year 1985, Kashmiri Muslims apology to Kashmiri hindus for their exodus, Britain's apology to India for subjugating it for 200 years, and India been recognised as the friend for all at the world stage.

Today being 15th August, I would like to mention the speech written by Sri Aurobindo for 15th August 1947. Perhaps this would inspire my countrymen.

[Sri Aurobindo wrote this message at the request of All India Radio, Tiruchirapalli, India, for broadcast on the eve of India's independence. This is the message which was broadcast on August 14, 1947. It is of special relevance and importance even now.]

August 15th, 1947 is the birthday of free India. It marks for her the end of an old era, the beginning of a new age. But we can also make it by our life and acts as a free nation an important date in a new age opening for the whole world, for the political, social, cultural and spiritual future of humanity.

August 15th is my own birthday and it is naturally gratifying to me that it should have assumed this vast significance. I take this coincidence, not as a fortuitous accident, but as the sanction and seal of the Divine Force that guides my steps on the work with which I began life, the beginning of its full fruition. Indeed, on this day I can watch almost all the world-movements which I hoped to see fulfilled in my lifetime, though then they looked like impracticable dreams, arriving at fruition or on their way to achievement. In all these movements free India may well play a large part and take a leading position.

The first of these dreams was a revolutionary movement which would create a free and united India. India today is free but she has not achieved unity. At one moment it almost seemed as if in the very act of liberation she would fall back into the chaos of separate States which preceded the British conquest. But fortunately it now seems probable that this danger will be averted and a large and powerful, though not yet a complete union will be established. Also, the wisely drastic policy of the Constituent Assembly has made it probable that the problem of the depressed classes will be solved without schism or fissure. But the old communal division into Hindus and Muslims seems now to have hardened into a permanent political division of the country. It is to be hoped that this settled fact will not be accepted as settled for ever or as anything more than a temporary expedient. For if it lasts, India may be seriously weakened, even crippled: civil strife may remain always possible, possible even a new invasion and foreign conquest. India's internal development and prosperity may be impeded, her position among the nations weakened, her destiny impaired or even frustrated. This must not be; the partition must go. Let us hope that that may come about naturally, by an increasing recognition of the necessity not only of peace and concord but of common action, by the practice of common action and the creation of means for that purpose. In this way unity may finally come about under whatever form—the exact form may have a pragmatic but not a fundamental importance. But by whatever means, in whatever way, the division must go; unity must and will be achieved, for it is necessary for the greatness of India's future.

Another dream was for the resurgence and liberation of the peoples of Asia and her return to her great role in the progress of human civilisation. Asia has arisen; large parts are now quite free or are at this moment being liberated: its other still subject or partly subject parts are moving through whatever struggles towards freedom. Only a little has to be done and that will be done today or tomorrow. There India has her part to play and has begun to play it with an energy and ability which already indicate the measure of her possibilities and the place she can take in the council of the nations.

The third dream was a world-union forming the outer basis of a fairer, brighter and nobler life for all mankind. That unification of the human world is under way; there is an imperfect initiation organised but struggling against tremendous difficulties. But the momentum is there and it must inevitably increase and conquer. Here too India has begun to play a prominent part and, if she can develop that larger statesmanship which is not limited by the present facts and immediate possibilities but looks into the future and brings it nearer, her presence may make all the difference between a slow and timid and a bold and swift development. A catastrophe may intervene and interrupt or destroy what is being done, but even then the final result is sure. For unification is a necessity of Nature, an inevitable movement. Its necessity for the nations is also clear, for without it the freedom of the small nations may be at any moment in peril and the life even of the large and *powerful nations insecure. The unification is therefore to the interests of all, and only human imbecility and stupid selfishness can prevent it; but these cannot stand forever against the necessity of Nature and the Divine Will. But an outward basis is not enough; there must grow an international spirit and outlook, international forms and institutions must appear, perhaps such developments as dual or multilateral citizenship, willed interchange or voluntary fusion of cultures. Nationalism will have fulfilled itself and lost its militancy and would no longer find these things incompatible with self-preservation and the integrality of its outlook. A new spirit of oneness will take hold of the human race.*

Another dream, the spiritual gift of India to the world has already begun. India's spirituality is entering Europe and America in an ever increasing measure. That movement will grow; amid the disasters of the time more and more eyes are turning towards her with hope and there is even an increasing resort not only to her teachings, but to her psychic and spiritual practice.

The final dream was a step in evolution which would raise man to a higher and larger consciousness and begin the solution of the problems which have perplexed and vexed him since he first began to think and to dream of individual perfection and a perfect society. This is still a personal hope and an idea, an ideal which has begun to take hold both in India and in the West on forward-looking minds. The difficulties in the way are more formidable than in any other field of endeavour, but difficulties were made to be overcome and if the Supreme Will is there, they will be overcome. Here too, if this evolution is to take place, since it must proceed through a growth of the spirit and the inner consciousness, the initiative can come from India and, although the scope must be universal, the central movement may be hers.

Such is the content which I put into this date of India's liberation; whether or how far this hope will be justified depends upon the new and free India.

Endnotes

This section contains the additional information which forms the basis for some of the chapters in this book. This section is divided into multiple sub-sections, like Spiritual, New Education Policy, Governance, and inputs which I received from others, etc.

These are taken from the internet, and moderated to some extent. The reader is encouraged to read these sections, contemplate, connect the dots, derive his/her own truth, and get inspiration to inspire others.

Religious & Spiritual Notes

This section contains the principle teachings from the holy books and from the God realized souls. The reader may see for himself/herself the commonality in these teachings, and derive conclusions.

The Bhagavad Gita

The Bhagavad Gita, often referred to simply as the Gita, is a 700-verse Hindu scripture that is part of the Indian epic Mahabharata. It is a dialogue between Arjuna and Shri Krishna, who serves as his charioteer. The Gita covers a wide range of philosophical and spiritual topics, but some of its main teachings include:

Duty and Dharma (Righteousness): One of the central themes of the Gita is the concept of duty (dharma). Shri Krishna advises Arjuna to fulfill his duties as a warrior, emphasizing the importance of performing one's duties selflessly and without attachment to the results.

Detachment and Renunciation: The Gita teaches the importance of detachment from the fruits of one's actions. Shri Krishna advises Arjuna to perform his duties without being attached to success or failure, pleasure or pain, and to renounce any sense of personal ownership over the outcomes.

Yoga and Self-realization: The Gita outlines various paths to spiritual realization, including Karma Yoga (the yoga of selfless action), Bhakti Yoga (the yoga of devotion), and Jnana Yoga (the yoga of knowledge).

These paths ultimately lead to self-realization and union with the divine.

Equality and Unity: Shri Krishna teaches that all beings are essentially divine and that there is an underlying unity that connects everything in the universe. He emphasizes the importance of treating all beings with equality and compassion.

Discipline and Control of the Mind: The Gita emphasizes the importance of discipline and control of the mind. Shri Krishna teaches Arjuna techniques for mastering the mind, such as meditation and dhyana, in order to attain inner peace and self-mastery.

Faith and Surrender: The Gita encourages faith in the divine and surrender to the will of God. Shri Krishna advises Arjuna to surrender his will to the divine will and to have faith that God will guide him on the right path.

Overall, the Bhagavad Gita provides a comprehensive guide to living a righteous and fulfilling life, while also offering profound insights into the nature of the self, the universe, and the divine. Its teachings have had a profound influence on Hindu philosophy and spirituality, as well as on the broader spiritual and philosophical traditions of the world.

Prophet Muhammad

The main teachings of Prophet Muhammad, as conveyed through the Quran and Hadith (sayings and actions attributed to him), encompass various aspects of faith, morality, spirituality, and social conduct. Here are some of the central teachings of Prophet Muhammad:

Monotheism (Tawhid): The primary message of Islam is the belief in the oneness of God (Allah). Prophet Muhammad emphasized the importance of monotheism and rejected polytheism, teaching that Allah is the sole creator, sustainer, and ruler of the universe.

Submission to the Will of God (Islam): The word "Islam" itself means submission to the will of God. Prophet Muhammad taught that true faith involves surrendering one's will to the divine and striving to live in accordance with God's commandments as revealed in the Quran.

Compassion and Mercy: Prophet Muhammad exemplified compassion and mercy in his interactions with others. He taught his followers to be kind, compassionate, and merciful towards all beings, regardless of their religion, race, or social status.

Justice and Equity: Prophet Muhammad emphasized the importance of justice and equity in all aspects of life. He taught that all individuals are equal in the eyes of God and should be treated fairly and justly. He advocated for the rights of the oppressed, the poor, and the marginalized.

Humility and Modesty: Prophet Muhammad lived a humble and modest life, despite his role as the leader of the Muslim community. He taught his followers to be humble and modest in their behavior and to avoid arrogance and pride.

Forgiveness and Patience: Prophet Muhammad emphasized the virtues of forgiveness and patience. He taught that forgiveness is a sign of strength, not weakness, and encouraged his followers to forgive those who wronged them. He also stressed the importance of patience in facing life's challenges and trials.

Brotherhood and Unity: Prophet Muhammad emphasized the importance of unity and brotherhood among Muslims. He taught that all Muslims are part of a single ummah (community) and should support and care for one another.

Prayer and Worship: Prophet Muhammad stressed the importance of regular prayer (salat) and worship as a means of connecting with God and seeking His guidance and blessings. He established the five daily prayers as a central pillar of Islamic practice.

These teachings of Prophet Muhammad continue to serve as guiding principles for Muslims around the world, shaping their beliefs, attitudes, and actions in all aspects of life.

Jesus Christ

The main teachings of Jesus Christ, as recorded in the New Testament of the Bible, revolve around themes of oneness of God, love, compassion, forgiveness, humility, and service. God is one and he is the most merciful. Here are some of the key teachings attributed to Jesus:

Love: Jesus emphasized the importance of love, teaching his followers to love one another as they love themselves. This includes loving one's neighbors, enemies, and even strangers.

Compassion: Jesus showed compassion towards the marginalized, the sick, and the oppressed. He taught his followers to do the same, urging them to care for those in need and to show mercy and kindness to all.

Forgiveness: Jesus preached forgiveness, encouraging his followers to forgive those who wrong them and to seek forgiveness for their own sins. He taught that forgiveness is essential for spiritual growth and healing.

Humility: Jesus exemplified humility throughout his life, teaching his followers to be humble and to prioritize service to others over personal ambition or pride.

Faith: Jesus emphasized the importance of faith in God and encouraged his followers to trust in God's love, provision, and guidance.

Repentance: Jesus called people to repentance, urging them to turn away from sin and to seek reconciliation with God. He taught that true repentance leads to spiritual renewal and transformation.

Eternal life: Jesus taught about the kingdom of God and the promise of eternal life for those who believe in him. He emphasized the importance of living in accordance with God's will in order to inherit eternal life.

These teachings form the foundation of Christian faith and are central to the beliefs and practices of Christians around the world. They continue to inspire individuals to live lives of love, compassion, and service today.

Guru Nanak dev ji

Guru Nanak, the founder of Sikhism, espoused several key teachings that form the foundation of Sikh philosophy. Here are some of the main teachings of Guru Nanak:

Oneness of God (Ik Onkar): Guru Nanak preached the belief in one formless, omnipresent, and eternal God, referred to as "Ik Onkar," meaning "One Creator." He emphasized that there is only one God who is the creator of the universe and exists in all creation.

Equality and Brotherhood: Guru Nanak strongly advocated for the equality of all human beings, regardless of caste, creed, gender, or social status. He emphasized the idea of human brotherhood, promoting love, compassion, and respect for all.

Service and Charity: Guru Nanak emphasized the importance of selfless service (seva) and charity (daan). He believed in helping those in need and serving the community as a way to express devotion to God.

Nam Simran (Meditation on God's Name): Guru Nanak stressed the significance of remembering and meditating on the divine name as a means to connect with God and attain spiritual enlightenment. The repetition of God's name (Naam Japna) is considered essential in Sikh practice.

Honest Living and Hard Work: Guru Nanak encouraged honest living and hard work as a means to sustain oneself and contribute positively to society. He rejected the notion of asceticism and emphasized the importance of leading a worldly life while remaining spiritually connected to God.

Rejecting Rituals and Superstitions: Guru Nanak criticized empty rituals, superstitions, and external religious practices devoid of true devotion and understanding. He emphasized inner purity, sincerity, and genuine devotion to God over superficial rituals.

Humility and Contentment: Guru Nanak taught the importance of humility (Nimrata) and contentment (Santosh) as virtues essential for spiritual growth. He emphasized the need to remain humble and satisfied with one's circumstances while striving for spiritual progress.

Unity of Humankind: Guru Nanak envisioned a world where people from different backgrounds coexist peacefully, embracing diversity while recognizing the unity of humankind. He spoke out against divisions and conflicts based on religious, social, or ethnic differences.

These teachings of Guru Nanak continue to guide and inspire millions of people in India, and around the world, shaping their spiritual beliefs and guiding their actions in daily life.

Gautam Budhha

Gautama Buddha, the founder of Buddhism, imparted various teachings that form the foundation of this spiritual tradition. Some of the main teachings of Gautama Buddha include:

The Four Noble Truths:

Dukkha (Suffering): Life is marked by suffering, dissatisfaction, or unsatisfactoriness.

Samudaya (Origin of Suffering): The cause of suffering is desire, craving, or attachment.

Nirodha (Cessation of Suffering): There is a way to end suffering by eliminating desire and attachment.

Magga (Path to the Cessation of Suffering): The Eightfold Path, a set of principles and practices that lead to the cessation of suffering.

The Noble Eightfold Path:

Right Understanding

Right Thought

Right Speech

Right Action

Right Livelihood

Right Effort

Right Mindfulness

Right Concentration

Impermanence (Anicca): The teaching that all things, including life itself, are impermanent and subject to change.

Non-Self (Anatta): The concept that there is no permanent, unchanging self or soul, but rather an ever-changing collection of elements.

Karma: The law of cause and effect, where actions have consequences, and ethical behavior leads to positive outcomes.

Compassion and Loving-Kindness (Metta): The importance of cultivating kindness, compassion, and empathy towards oneself and others.

Mindfulness (Sati): Being fully aware and present in each moment, observing thoughts, feelings, and sensations without attachment or judgment.

These teachings emphasize the importance of ethical conduct, mental discipline, and wisdom in overcoming suffering and attaining enlightenment (Nirvana).

Vardhaman Mahavir

Vardhaman Mahavir, also known simply as Mahavir or Lord Mahavira, was the 24th Tirthankara (a revered teacher) of Jainism, an ancient Indian religion. His teachings are primarily encapsulated in the principles of Jainism, which emphasize non-violence (Ahimsa), truthfulness (Satya), non-stealing (Asteya), celibacy (Brahmacharya), and non-possession or non-attachment (Aparigraha). Here are some of the main teachings associated with Mahavir:

Ahimsa (Non-violence): This is one of the core principles of Jainism. Mahavir emphasized the importance of avoiding harm to any living being, whether it's humans, animals, or even plants. This principle extends beyond physical violence to include mental and verbal harm as well.

Satya (Truthfulness): Mahavir stressed the importance of truthfulness in thought, word, and action. Followers of Jainism are encouraged to always speak the truth and live a life that aligns with honesty and integrity.

Asteya (Non-stealing): Asteya refers to refraining from stealing or taking anything that does not belong to you without permission. Mahavir taught that followers should earn their living through honest means and avoid taking what rightfully belongs to others.

Brahmacharya (Celibacy): This principle emphasizes self-restraint and control over one's desires, particularly in the context of sexual conduct. Mahavir advocated for celibacy as a means to overcome worldly attachments and distractions.

Aparigraha (Non-possession/Non-attachment): Aparigraha teaches detachment from material possessions and worldly attachments. Mahavir believed that true liberation could only be attained by letting go of desires for material wealth and possessions.

Anekantavada (Principle of Non-absolutism): Mahavir also promoted the concept of Anekantavada, which acknowledges the multiplicity of perspectives and the idea that truth is multifaceted. This principle encourages tolerance, understanding, and respect for differing viewpoints.

Karma Doctrine: Like many Indian philosophical traditions, Jainism subscribes to the concept of karma. Mahavir taught that every action, whether physical, verbal, or mental, has consequences that affect one's future experiences. Through ethical living and spiritual practices, individuals can purify their karma and progress towards spiritual liberation.

Mahavir's teachings emphasize the cultivation of inner peace, ethical conduct, and spiritual liberation through self-discipline and non-violence. His teachings continue to inspire millions of followers of Jainism and others alike, around the world.

Swami Vivekananda

Swami Vivekananda (1863–1902), one of India's most revered spiritual leaders and thinkers, made significant contributions to both the revitalization of Hindu philosophy and the promotion of interfaith dialogue and understanding. His teachings continue to inspire millions worldwide, and his influence extends far beyond his lifetime. Here's an overview of his contributions and some prominent individuals who were influenced by his guidance:

Revival of Hinduism: Swami Vivekananda played a pivotal role in revitalizing Hinduism and bringing its principles and practices to a global audience. He emphasized the universality of Hindu philosophy and its relevance to modern life. Vivekananda's speeches at the Parliament of the World's Religions in Chicago in 1893 introduced Hinduism to the Western world and garnered widespread acclaim. His teachings emphasized the harmony of religions and the importance of spiritual realization over dogma or ritual.

Propagation of Vedanta: Swami Vivekananda was a passionate advocate for Vedanta, the philosophical foundation of Hinduism that emphasizes the unity of all existence and the divinity of the soul. He popularized Vedantic teachings through his lectures, writings, and personal example, inspiring countless individuals to explore the depths of their own spirituality. Vivekananda's interpretation of Vedanta emphasized its practical application in daily life and its relevance to social reform and service.

Promotion of Service: Swami Vivekananda believed in the importance of selfless service as a means of realizing one's spiritual potential and alleviating the suffering of others. He founded the Ramakrishna Mission and the Ramakrishna Math, organizations dedicated to humanitarian work, education, and spiritual upliftment. Vivekananda's teachings on karma yoga (the yoga of selfless action) inspired many to dedicate themselves to serving humanity with compassion and humility.

Empowerment of Youth: Swami Vivekananda had a profound impact on the youth of India, inspiring them to cultivate self-confidence, self-reliance, and a sense of national pride. His famous speech at the Parliament of the World's Religions, beginning with the words "Sisters and Brothers of America," resonated deeply with young Indians and instilled in them a sense of cultural pride and identity.

Vivekananda's teachings on self-discipline, courage, and perseverance continue to inspire youth around the world to strive for excellence and contribute positively to society.

Prominent Individuals Influenced by Vivekananda:

Mahatma Gandhi: Mahatma Gandhi, the leader of India's nonviolent independence movement, was deeply influenced by Swami Vivekananda's teachings on truth, nonviolence, and service. Gandhi regarded Vivekananda as his spiritual mentor and drew inspiration from his writings and speeches.

Sister Nivedita: Sister Nivedita, a disciple of Swami Vivekananda, dedicated her life to the service of India and its people. She played a key role in promoting education, women's empowerment, and social reform, following Vivekananda's ideals of selfless service and spiritual activism.

Jamsetji Tata: Jamsetji Tata, the founder of the Tata Group, was inspired by Swami Vivekananda's vision of a resurgent India and his emphasis on education, innovation, and social responsibility. Tata's philanthropic endeavors, including the establishment of educational institutions and research centers, were influenced by Vivekananda's teachings on nation-building and economic self-sufficiency.

Swami Vivekananda's legacy as a spiritual leader, social reformer, and advocate for universal values continues to inspire people of all backgrounds and cultures. His teachings on the unity of religions, the divinity of the human soul, and the power of selfless service remain relevant in addressing the challenges of the modern world and promoting harmony, compassion, and understanding among all people.

Sri Aurobindo (1872-1950)

Sri Aurobindo, a prominent Indian philosopher, yogi, and nationalist leader, played a significant role in both the Indian freedom movement and spiritual upliftment. As an influential figure in the early 20th century, he emerged as a fierce advocate for India's independence from British colonial rule. Aurobindo utilized his intellectual prowess and oratory skills to galvanize the masses, advocating for self-reliance, cultural rejuvenation, and political sovereignty. His fiery speeches and writings inspired a generation of freedom fighters and nationalists, earning him admiration and respect across the Indian subcontinent.

Sri Aurobindo's contributions to the Indian freedom movement began to crystallize during his years in England, where he pursued higher studies. Exposed to Western philosophical and political thought, he developed a keen interest in nationalist ideals. However, it was upon his return to India in 1893 that Sri Aurobindo's political activism gained momentum. He joined the Indian National Congress and actively engaged in the discourse surrounding India's liberation from British colonial rule.

Sri Aurobindo's role in the Indian freedom struggle manifested through his prolific writings and oratory skills. He became the editor of the nationalist newspaper "Bande Mataram," using it as a platform to propagate his revolutionary ideas. His stirring articles and speeches galvanized the Indian masses, urging them to break free from the shackles of British imperialism. Sri Aurobindo's nationalist fervor and intellectual acumen positioned him as one of the leading voices advocating for complete independence from British rule.

However, Sri Aurobindo's contributions were not limited to the political arena. In 1908, following his arrest in connection with revolutionary activities, he underwent a transformative spiritual experience while imprisoned. This profound awakening marked a significant turning point in his life, leading him to shift his focus from political activism to spiritual exploration.

Sri Aurobindo's spiritual journey took him deep into the realms of yoga and mysticism. He synthesized Eastern and Western spiritual philosophies, drawing inspiration from sources as diverse as the Gita, Upanishads, Vedanta, and the works of Western philosophers like Plato and Nietzsche. Sri Aurobindo's Integral Yoga philosophy emphasized the evolution of consciousness and the realization of divine potential within each individual.

In 1910, Sri Aurobindo withdrew from public life and settled in Pondicherry, then a French colony, to pursue his spiritual practices in seclusion. There, his spiritual companion The Mother founded the Sri Aurobindo Ashram, which would become a vibrant spiritual community attracting seekers from around the world. Sri Aurobindo's teachings, disseminated through his numerous writings and personal guidance, inspired a new approach to spirituality—one that integrated the pursuit of inner transformation with active engagement in the world.

Central to Sri Aurobindo's vision was the concept of the "divine life," wherein individuals seek to align their thoughts, actions, and aspirations with the divine will. He articulated this vision in works such as "The Life Divine" and "Essays on the Gita," which expound upon the integral unity of existence and the evolutionary journey of consciousness towards its ultimate fulfillment.

Paramhansa Yogananda (1893 - 1952)

Paramahansa Yogananda, a revered spiritual teacher and founder of the Self-Realization Fellowship (SRF), and Yogoda Satsang Society (YSS) of India, made profound contributions to the dissemination of yoga and meditation practices in the US (and west), particularly in the 20th century. Born Mukunda Lal Ghosh in 1893 in India, Yogananda displayed a deep inclination towards spirituality from a young age. He became a disciple of Swami Sri Yukteswar Giri and later embarked on a mission to introduce the ancient teachings of yoga to the Western world.

Paramhansa Yogananda's most significant contribution lies in his popularization of Kriya Yoga, a spiritual discipline aimed at attaining self-realization through meditation, self-discipline, and the awakening of the subtle energies within the body. His seminal work, "Autobiography of a Yogi," published in 1946, became a bestseller and introduced millions of readers worldwide to the principles of yoga and meditation. The book continues to inspire seekers on the spiritual path and has been translated into numerous languages.

One of the most prominent individuals who gained from Yogananda's guidance was George Harrison, the lead guitarist of The Beatles. Harrison, known for his interest in Eastern spirituality, credited Yogananda's teachings as a significant influence on his spiritual journey. Harrison's encounter with "Autobiography of a Yogi" sparked a lifelong interest in yoga and meditation, shaping his personal and creative pursuits.

Another notable figure influenced by Paramhansa Yogananda was Mahatma Gandhi, the leader of India's nonviolent independence movement. While Mahatma Gandhi's spiritual path differed from Yogananda's, he expressed admiration for the yogi's teachings and acknowledged the role of spiritual practices in his life and leadership. Yogananda's message of universal love and harmony resonated with Mahatma Gandhi's philosophy of Ahimsa (nonviolence) and Sarvodaya (welfare of all).

Neeb Karori Baba (1900 - 1973)

Neem Karoli Baba, also known as Maharaj-ji, was a revered saint and spiritual teacher who gained widespread recognition for his simple yet profound teachings and his embodiment of unconditional love and compassion. Born in 1900 in the village of Akbarpur in Uttar Pradesh, India, he displayed spiritual inclinations from a young age. Neem Karoli Baba's teachings transcended religious boundaries and attracted followers from various backgrounds, including Hindus, Muslims, Christians, and Western seekers.

One of the most prominent individuals who gained from Neem Karoli Baba's guidance was Ram Dass, formerly known as Richard Alpert, a Harvard psychologist and pioneer of the psychedelic movement in the 1960s. Ram Dass's encounter with Neem Karoli Baba in India proved to be a life-changing experience, leading him to embark on a spiritual journey that transformed his understanding of consciousness and the nature of reality. Ram Dass became a devoted disciple of Maharaj-ji and played a pivotal role in introducing his teachings to the West through his books and lectures, including the bestselling "Be Here Now."

Another influential figure touched by Neem Karoli Baba's grace was Steve Jobs, the co-founder of Apple Inc. Jobs traveled to India in the 1970s in search of spiritual wisdom and had a profound encounter with Maharaj-ji. Although Jobs did not spend an extensive amount of time with Neem Karoli Baba, the encounter left an indelible mark on him, shaping his approach to life and work. Jobs often spoke of the importance of intuition and spiritual intuition in his creative process, a perspective he credited to his experiences in India.

Neem Karoli Baba's teachings emphasized the universality of love and the importance of selfless service (seva) as a means of attaining spiritual realization. He often encouraged his followers to cultivate faith (shraddha) and surrender (saranagati) to the divine will, teaching that true freedom lies in surrendering the ego and aligning oneself with the flow of grace.

Neem Karoli Baba's influence extended far beyond his physical presence, as stories of his miracles and compassionate deeds continue to inspire countless individuals around the world. His ashrams in India, particularly the Kainchi Dham ashram in Uttarakhand, serve as centers of spiritual practice and pilgrimage for devotees seeking solace and guidance.

In conclusion, Neem Karoli Baba's teachings continue to resonate with seekers on the spiritual path, transcending cultural and religious boundaries. Through his example of unconditional love, compassion, and selfless service, he touched the lives of countless individuals, including prominent figures in various fields. His legacy endures as a testament to the transformative power of love and devotion in the quest for spiritual awakening.

NEP 2020

New Education Policy 2020 represents a significant paradigm shift in the Indian education system, emphasizing learner-centric, holistic, and flexible approaches to education. It seeks to empower learners with the knowledge, skills, and values necessary to thrive in a rapidly changing world while promoting inclusivity, equity, and social cohesion. However, the successful implementation of NEP 2020 will require concerted efforts from all stakeholders, including policymakers, educators, parents, and civil society organizations.

Sri Aurobindo's philosophy and vision of education have had a significant influence on the New Education Policy (NEP) 2020, particularly in shaping its holistic and integral approach to education. While Sri Aurobindo's direct influence on the policy may not be explicitly mentioned, his ideas on education, consciousness, and human potential have informed the broader discourse on educational reform in India. Here are some ways in which Sri Aurobindo's influence can be seen in NEP 2020:

Holistic Development: Sri Aurobindo emphasized the integral development of the individual, encompassing physical, mental, emotional, and spiritual dimensions. Similarly, NEP 2020 advocates for a holistic approach to education that goes beyond academic learning to promote the overall well-being and development of learners. The policy emphasizes the importance of nurturing cognitive, socio-emotional, and physical skills, aligning with Sri Aurobindo's vision of integral education.

Integration of Arts and Culture: Sri Aurobindo stressed the importance of integrating arts, culture, and values into education to foster creativity, imagination, and ethical values. NEP 2020 emphasizes the preservation and promotion of India's linguistic and cultural heritage, advocating for the study of Indian languages, arts, and culture at all levels of education. This emphasis on cultural integration and value-based education resonates with Sri Aurobindo's vision of education as a means of spiritual and cultural regeneration.

Development of Higher Consciousness: Sri Aurobindo's philosophy of education emphasizes the development of higher levels of consciousness and the realization of the divine potential within each individual. While NEP 2020 may not explicitly mention spiritual development, its emphasis on promoting critical thinking, creativity, and ethical values aligns with the broader goal of fostering the holistic development of learners and awakening their inner potential.

Flexibility and Adaptability: Sri Aurobindo emphasized the need for education to be flexible and adaptable to the evolving needs of society and the individual. NEP 2020 advocates for a flexible curriculum framework that promotes multidisciplinary learning, experiential learning, and vocational education from an early age. The policy also emphasizes the importance of lifelong learning and skill development to empower individuals to thrive in a rapidly changing world.

Role of Teachers: Sri Aurobindo regarded teachers as spiritual guides and mentors who play a crucial role in nurturing the holistic development of learners. NEP 2020 emphasizes the importance of teacher training, continuous professional development, and autonomy to empower educators to create enriching learning experiences for their students. This recognition of the pivotal role of teachers aligns with Sri Aurobindo's vision of education as a collaborative and transformative process guided by enlightened educators.

Similarly, Swami Vivekananda, a towering figure in India's spiritual and educational landscape, has had a profound influence on the New Education Policy (NEP) 2020. His vision of education as a holistic and transformative process aimed at the development of the whole individual has resonated deeply with policymakers and educators shaping the policy. Here are some ways in which Swami Vivekananda's influence can be seen in NEP 2020:

Emphasis on Holistic Development: Swami Vivekananda emphasized the holistic development of individuals, encompassing physical, mental, emotional, and spiritual dimensions. Similarly, NEP 2020 advocates for a holistic approach to education that goes beyond academic learning to foster the overall well-being and development of learners. The policy emphasizes the importance of nurturing cognitive, socio-emotional, and physical skills, aligning with Swami Vivekananda's vision of integral education.

Promotion of Values and Ethics: Swami Vivekananda stressed the importance of moral and ethical values in education, advocating for the cultivation of character and virtue alongside intellectual growth. NEP 2020 similarly emphasizes the promotion of ethical and human values, aiming to instill in students a sense of responsibility, empathy, and social justice. The policy underscores the importance of value-based education to nurture responsible citizenship and ethical leadership.

Role of Teachers as Mentors: Swami Vivekananda regarded teachers as spiritual guides and mentors who play a crucial role in shaping the character and destiny of their students. NEP 2020 recognizes the pivotal role of teachers in the educational process and emphasizes the importance of teacher training, continuous professional development, and autonomy. The policy aims to empower educators to create enriching learning experiences and serve as positive role models for their students.

Integration of Science and Spirituality: Swami Vivekananda advocated for the integration of science and spirituality in education, emphasizing the harmony between rational inquiry and spiritual wisdom. NEP 2020 recognizes the importance of integrating scientific knowledge with traditional wisdom and indigenous knowledge systems. The policy promotes interdisciplinary approaches to learning, encouraging students to explore the intersections between science, technology, culture, and spirituality.

Promotion of Universal Education: Swami Vivekananda was a passionate advocate for universal education and believed that education should be accessible to all, regardless of gender, caste, or socioeconomic status. NEP 2020 aims to promote equity, inclusion, and access to quality education for all learners, with a particular focus on marginalized and disadvantaged groups. The policy advocates for the removal of barriers to education and the expansion of educational opportunities to ensure that every child has the chance to realize their full potential.

Indices for better Governance

Proposed below are some assessment indices which can be coupled with the already present indices, to improve the governance systems and improve accountability. These were briefly discussed in my book, "Discovery of New India", published in 2021. Here I am expanding these, taking inputs from the internet.

PIN code Sufficiency Index (PSI)

This index is about checking the demand and supply of services and government amenities at the PIN code level. Every PIN code should be rated by the citizens for the services and amenities that they receive from the local, state and the central governments. PSI at city, district and state level can help identify the laggard departments, and help them scaleup.

Creating a PIN code Sufficiency Index for a town's redevelopment involves evaluating various factors to determine the sufficiency and potential for improvement within each PIN code area. Here are some elements that could be included:

Demographic Data: Factors such as population density, age distribution, income levels, education levels, and household composition can provide insights into the socio-economic landscape of each PIN code.

Economic Indicators: Include metrics such as employment rates, median household income, poverty levels, and the presence of businesses to assess economic vitality and potential for growth.

Housing Availability and Affordability: Evaluate housing stock, vacancy rates, median rent and home prices, and affordability indices to understand housing conditions and challenges within each PIN code.

Infrastructure and Transportation: Assess the quality of infrastructure such as roads, public transportation options, access to healthcare facilities, and proximity to essential services like grocery stores and banks.

Education and Skill Development: Include metrics related to the quality of schools, graduation rates, access to vocational training programs, and availability of higher education institutions.

Health and Well-being: Factors such as access to healthcare services, rates of chronic diseases, availability of recreational facilities, and air and water quality can provide insights into the overall health and well-being of residents.

Community Engagement and Civic Participation: Evaluate levels of community engagement, presence of community organizations, access to public spaces, and participation in local governance.

Environmental Sustainability: Assess factors such as green spaces, recycling programs, renewable energy adoption, and efforts towards sustainability and resilience.

Crime and Safety: Include crime rates, presence of law enforcement agencies, and community safety initiatives to gauge the level of safety within each PIN code.

Technology and Connectivity: Evaluate access to high-speed internet, digital literacy rates, availability of technology resources, and innovation hubs to understand the technological infrastructure and potential for digital inclusion.

Historical and Cultural Significance: Consider the preservation of historical sites, cultural institutions, and efforts to promote diversity and inclusion within each PIN code.

Government Support and Policy Environment: Assess the availability of government resources, incentive programs for redevelopment, zoning regulations, and policies supporting economic and community development.

By compiling and analyzing data across these categories, a "PIN code Sufficiency Index" can provide a comprehensive understanding of the strengths, weaknesses, and opportunities for redevelopment within each area, guiding strategic planning and investment decisions for the town's revitalization efforts.

Industry Pollution Index (IPI)

Uncontrolled industrial production has resulted in the pollution of air, water and soil. Existing measures of Pollution Index (PI) are not able to control the problem. Lakhs of organized factory units, and many more lakhs unorganized factories are escaping the periodic scrutiny. In fact, it is important to reassess the industries in totality, i.e. for their end-to-end functioning – from receiving raw materials to finished product, including by-products and most importantly their waste. Regulators should critically look at the waste disposal mechanisms. Government should make a mechanism for effective waste disposal.

Every unit should be recertified as per the revised norms, IPI scores to be published, incentives should be given to greener units. Governments and authorities should help other units become green within 5 years. Non-green factories to be shut-down in 5 years. This will push the industries to become green in 5 years.

The "Industry Pollution Index" can be a comprehensive metric that encompasses various factors contributing to pollution from industrial activities in urban areas. Here are some components that can be included:

Air Pollution Emissions: Measurement of emissions of various pollutants such as sulfur dioxide (SO_2), nitrogen oxides (NOx), particulate matter (PM), volatile organic compounds (VOCs), and carbon monoxide (CO) from industrial sources.

Water Pollution: Assessment of effluent discharges into water bodies including rivers, lakes, and oceans.

This can include pollutants such as heavy metals, chemicals, and organic matter.

Land Pollution: Evaluation of industrial waste disposal practices including solid waste, hazardous waste, and contaminated landfills. Monitoring soil contamination from industrial activities.

Noise Pollution: Monitoring noise levels generated by industrial machinery, transportation of goods, and other industrial processes.

Energy Consumption: Tracking energy usage by industries and promoting energy-efficient practices to reduce emissions associated with energy production.

Waste Management Practices: Assessing the effectiveness of waste management strategies such as recycling, reuse, and proper disposal of industrial waste products.

Compliance with Environmental Regulations: Ensuring that industries adhere to environmental regulations and standards set by regulatory authorities regarding emissions, waste disposal, and pollution control measures.

Environmental Impact Assessments: Conducting regular assessments to determine the environmental impact of industrial activities on surrounding ecosystems, biodiversity, and human health.

Green Technologies Adoption: Encouraging industries to adopt cleaner production technologies, renewable energy sources, and sustainable practices to minimize pollution.

Public Health Indicators: Monitoring health outcomes in nearby communities to assess the impact of industrial pollution on public health, including respiratory diseases, cardiovascular problems, and cancer rates.

Community Engagement and Transparency: Involving local communities in decision-making processes regarding industrial development, pollution control measures, and environmental monitoring to foster transparency and accountability.

Emergency Preparedness and Response: Developing contingency plans and response mechanisms to address industrial accidents, spills, or other incidents that may result in pollution and environmental damage.

By incorporating these elements into the Industry Pollution Index, policymakers, regulatory agencies, and industries can effectively monitor and mitigate pollution levels in urban areas, promoting sustainable development and improving overall environmental quality.

Department's Honesty Index (DHI)

All government departments, which are not able to crush corruption, are to be rated by the citizens/public dealing with them. Feedback using a transparent feedback system should be published. Published department honesty index DHI will shame the corrupt departments. This should be linked with government aids and promotions. Thus, it will promote healthy competition among the department chiefs and ministries, they will make efforts to become more honest.

Creating a "Department's Honesty Index" involves establishing a set of criteria and metrics to evaluate the transparency and honesty of a government department. Here are some components that could be included in such an index:

Disclosure Policies: Evaluate the department's policies regarding the disclosure of information to the public. This includes the frequency and completeness of reports, datasets, and other relevant information made available to the public.

Transparency of Decision-making Processes: Assess how transparent the department is in its decision-making processes. This could include public consultations, open meetings, and clear documentation of decision-making criteria.

Accessibility of Information: Measure how easily accessible the department's information is to the general public. This includes the usability of the department's website, availability of information in multiple languages, and efforts to make information accessible to people with disabilities.

Whistleblower Protection: Evaluate the department's policies and practices related to protecting whistleblowers who report wrongdoing or unethical behavior within the department.

Conflict of Interest Policies: Assess the department's policies and procedures for identifying and managing conflicts of interest among its staff and leadership.

Response to Public Inquiries: Measure the department's responsiveness to public inquiries and requests for information. This includes the timeliness and completeness of responses to inquiries from the public, media, and other stakeholders.

Compliance with Open Data Standards: Evaluate the department's compliance with open data standards and initiatives, ensuring that data is provided in formats that are accessible, machine-readable, and reusable.

Ethics Training and Awareness: Assess the department's efforts to promote ethics training and awareness among its staff, including training programs, ethical guidelines, and codes of conduct.

Public Feedback Mechanisms: Evaluate the department's mechanisms for soliciting and responding to feedback from the public, such as public forums, surveys, and complaint mechanisms.

External Oversight and Accountability: Consider the presence and effectiveness of external oversight bodies, such as auditors, ombudsmen, or independent review panels, tasked with monitoring the department's transparency and honesty.

By creating a comprehensive index that encompasses these elements, a government department can enhance transparency and accountability, ultimately fostering public trust and confidence in its operations.

Natural Resources Preservation Index (NRPI)

Creating a "Natural Resources Preservation Index" involves assessing various factors related to the conservation and sustainable use of natural resources in a particular place. Here are some elements that could be included in such an index:

Biodiversity: Measure the diversity and abundance of plant and animal species in the area. This could include assessing the presence of endangered species, endemic species, and the overall health of ecosystems.

Habitat Protection: Evaluate the extent and effectiveness of protected areas such as national parks, nature reserves, and wildlife sanctuaries. Consider the size, connectivity, and management of these areas.

Forest Cover: Assess the extent and health of forests, including both natural and planted forests. Look at forest loss and gain, deforestation rates, and the implementation of sustainable forestry practices.

Water Quality and Quantity: Monitor the quality and availability of water resources such as rivers, lakes, and groundwater. Look at factors like pollution levels, water extraction rates, and the implementation of water conservation measures.

Air Quality: Evaluate air pollution levels, particularly concentrations of pollutants like particulate matter, ozone, sulfur dioxide, and nitrogen oxides. Assess the impact of human activities such as industrial emissions, transportation, and agriculture.

Soil Health: Assess soil quality and fertility, including factors such as soil erosion, contamination, and nutrient depletion. Consider the implementation of soil conservation practices and sustainable agricultural methods.

Carbon Footprint: Measure greenhouse gas emissions from various sources such as energy production, transportation, industry, and land use changes. Evaluate efforts to reduce emissions and increase carbon sequestration through initiatives like reforestation and afforestation.

Renewable Energy Usage: Evaluate the adoption of renewable energy sources such as solar, wind, hydroelectric, and geothermal power. Consider the proportion of energy generated from renewable sources and the implementation of policies to promote renewable energy deployment.

Waste Management: Assess waste generation rates, recycling rates, and the implementation of waste reduction and recycling programs. Evaluate efforts to minimize landfilling and promote composting and resource recovery.

Environmental Policies and Governance: Evaluate the strength and effectiveness of environmental policies, regulations, and enforcement mechanisms at the local, regional, and national levels. Consider factors such as environmental laws, institutional capacity, stakeholder engagement, and public awareness.

By combining these factors into an index, policymakers, researchers, and stakeholders can gain insights into the state of natural resource preservation in a particular place and track progress over time.

History and Culture Preservation Index (HCPI)

The "History and Culture Preservation Index" for a place could encompass various factors that contribute to the preservation, promotion, and understanding of its historical and cultural heritage. Here are some potential components that could be included:

Historical Sites and Monuments: Number and significance of historical landmarks, monuments, and sites preserved within the area.

Museum and Gallery Density: Number and diversity of museums, galleries, and cultural institutions showcasing the region's history and cultural artifacts.

Cultural Events and Festivals: Frequency and variety of cultural events, festivals, and celebrations that showcase local traditions, arts, and heritage.

Archives and Libraries: Availability and accessibility of archives, libraries, and historical records documenting the region's past.

Cultural Education Programs: Presence of educational programs, workshops, and initiatives aimed at educating the community and visitors about local history and culture.

Heritage Conservation Policies: Strength and effectiveness of government policies and initiatives aimed at preserving and protecting historical sites, buildings, and cultural traditions.

Community Engagement: Level of community involvement and participation in preserving and promoting local history and culture, including volunteer efforts and grassroots initiatives.

Cultural Diversity and Inclusivity: Recognition and promotion of diverse cultural heritage within the region, including efforts to include marginalized or underrepresented communities in the narrative of local history.

Tourism Impact: Sustainable management of tourism to historical and cultural sites, ensuring that tourism contributes positively to preservation efforts without causing damage or disruption.

Digital Preservation Efforts: Utilization of digital technologies and platforms for the documentation, preservation, and dissemination of historical and cultural information.

Historical Interpretation and Storytelling: Quality and accessibility of interpretive materials, guided tours, and storytelling efforts that help visitors understand the significance of historical and cultural sites.

Conservation of Traditional Crafts and Practices: Support for artisans and practitioners of traditional crafts and cultural practices, ensuring their continuation and transmission to future generations.

Local Heritage Products: Development and promotion of local products, handicrafts, and goods that are tied to the region's history and culture, supporting economic sustainability while preserving heritage.

Recognition and Awards: Recognition from national or international organizations for outstanding efforts in historical and cultural preservation.

Public Perception and Awareness: Surveys or assessments of public awareness, appreciation, and engagement with the region's history and cultural heritage.

These are just some examples, and the specific components of the index could vary depending on the context and priorities of the place being assessed.

Collaboration Index (to resolve interstate issues like Cauvery water issues) (CI).

Assessing the "Collaboration Index" between two adjacent states involves evaluating various aspects of their interaction and cooperation. Here are some factors that can be included to assess the Collaboration Index:

Joint Projects: Evaluate the number and scale of joint projects undertaken by the two states. This could include infrastructure development, environmental initiatives, cultural events, etc.

Economic Interdependence: Analyze the economic ties between the states, such as shared industries, trade volume, cross-border employment, and business partnerships.

Policy Alignment: Assess the degree to which the states' policies align and support each other's objectives, especially in areas such as urban planning, transportation, and environmental regulations.

Cross-Border Services: Evaluate the provision of services that benefit residents of both states, such as shared public transportation systems, healthcare facilities, or emergency response services.

Collaborative Institutions: Examine the presence and effectiveness of organizations or committees dedicated to fostering collaboration between the states, such as joint councils, task forces, or economic development boards.

Cultural Exchange: Measure the level of cultural exchange and cooperation through events, festivals, educational programs, and other initiatives aimed at promoting mutual understanding and appreciation.

Data Sharing and Research: Consider the extent to which the states share data and collaborate on research initiatives related to common challenges or opportunities, such as climate change adaptation, economic development, or public health.

Infrastructure Connectivity: Assess the quality and extent of infrastructure connecting the two states, including roads, bridges, railways, and utilities, and evaluate any joint efforts to improve connectivity.

Environmental Collaboration: Evaluate collaborative efforts to address shared environmental concerns, such as air and water quality, waste management, and conservation of natural resources.

Social Integration: Measure the level of social integration between the residents of the two cities, including inter-state events, community programs, and initiatives to promote social cohesion and inclusivity.

By considering these factors and possibly others relevant to the specific context of the state in question, you can develop a comprehensive assessment of their Collaboration Index.

State-level Indexes (SLIs)

Above indices will club to district level and further to state level. This will help in rating of states. Thus, it will promote healthy competition among the state chiefs and ministries for better performance of the states. Hence, a better India!

Compilation of the wishes some of my knowns have for India, for the next 10 years.

Universal brotherhood 

Environment

Jal sanchay, Van sanrakshan, Population control.

Measures to improve water table + forest cover.

Clear 20 Year Plan for protection of our mother nature/ Planet earth (It has to be Measurable and data to be available for all).

Grow forest cover around every urban city/semi urban centre by at least 100% of current forest percentage.

Education

Better education and medical facilities in Government institutions.

Common Education System PAN India (Diversity can be taken in account).

Universal Education - if needed reduce defence budget by half percent, but divert that budget to upgrade each govt school to raise their standard, establish a chain of teachers training institute (IITD-Indian Institute of Teacher Development). Each kid below 15 should be in the school system, any school.

Make military service for 5 years mandatory with (right to call as reserve for life) for entry into government jobs.

Health

Improve the health system; all hospitals and clinics should be taken over and run by the government for at least next 30 years.

Upgrade government hospitals and education systems to world class. Strict policy to comply with the standards and heavy penalty for non compliance.

Universal Health - with universal health card for each Indian registered on NRC, using which any citizen can walk in any health facility and get treated. Cost to be born by Insurance, premium for which born by govt. And funded through a health cess on luxury goods, liquor, cigarettes etc. Also will be needed is establishing new 100 mini-AIIMS every year with each having a batch of 100 medical seats.

Agriculture

More economic benefits for farmers.

Remove ceiling from ownership of agricultural land.

Remove mandatory Mandi system for farmers.

As of now we are almost a Surplus country...from here we can move towards organic farming (It's a huge task but if there is Leadership then next 30 years would be enough).

Social security

Social security and medical facilities for citizens and their families who have paid taxes for at least 15 years in a defined proportion of taxes paid.

Senior citizens are happy with facilities, amenities and pension rise.

Judiciary

Independent Judiciary. Improve the Judiciary system … people will not respect law till justice is served on time.

Common man's lack of faith in judiciary even after 75 years of independence has been its failure. Need a fair, fast and non corrupt judicial system.

Law and order must be tightened. Criminals face consequences irrespective of identity. This is the most important step.

Judiciary reforms to speed up case resolution- establish more courts and a process to result in more number of judges coming out on merit basis. Digitization and maintaining history of all cases online where the time taken can be instantly tracked. Increase the number of working days of courts.

Judgement in any court case shall have to be delivered based on number of witnesses *2 days + fifteen days to write the verdict.+ one month for initiating the case.

Make tax evasions a criminal offence and ensure strict compliance.

Introduce concept of penal compensation in Indian Jurisprudence on breach of contract.

Governance

Prepare the next level of leadership in all fields... infrastructure development, external affairs, law n order.

Continuing to focus on connectivity, good governance and investments in defence, it's time to use the strong resource pool by creating opportunities which multiply the growth rate; generate jobs and make India a manufacturing hub for the world.

Ultra modernization of all state police forces. Establish a network of forensics labs and Training of police officers. Full digitization of police stations and establish a network of all of them. Establish a nationwide database of criminals. Collect ID and biometrics of each person detained or arrested and add them to the database.

Implement UCC, NRC, CAA and implement a population policy that anyone having more than 2 kids will not be eligible for Govt. Subsidy, govt job, or Reservation

Establish a Canals network to connect all major rivers and canals to be wide and deep enough to support water transportation.

Electoral

Honest election. Honest Governance at each level.

Elections at all three levels should happen at the same time.

Right to vote needs to be limited to at least 12th pass citizens so that the country elects wisely and not through threat, influence or force.

Eligibility criteria to get elected needs to be at least graduation and to become a minister, chief minister or prime minister one needs to be a postgraduate.

References and Inspirations

[1] Complete Works of Sri Aurobindo, and The Mother
https://incarnateword.in/cwsa
https://motherandsriaurobindo.in/The-Mother/books/cwm/

[2] Dr. APJ Abdul Kalam, *Ignited Minds*, Penguin books India, 2002.

[3] Paramhansa Yogananda, *Autobiography of a Yogi,* YSS India, 1946.

[4] Maria Wirth, *Thank You India,* Garuda Prakashan, 2018.

[5] Swami Rama, *Living with the Himalayan Masters,* Himalayan Institute India, 2019.

[6] Ram Dass, *The Miracle of Love - Stories about Neem Karoli Baba*, Hanuman Foundation, 1995.

[7] Raboo Joshi, *I and my Father are One: The grand unification*, Rabindra Kumar Joshi, 2011.

[8] Vaibhav, *Discovery of New India*, Notion Press, 2021.

[9] Edited by Arif Akhtar Naqvi, *Baal Biradari - dedicated to Late Quaiser Naqvi sahab*, Creative Star Publications, 2022.

[10] Personal Spiritual experiences, 2020-2024.

[11] Jesus in India, Paramhansa Yogananda and other references.

[12] Wishes for India that some of my acquaintances shared with me, captured in the Endnotes.

About Author

Vaibhav comes from an educated middle-class Indian family. He is an engineer by education and profession. After spending about 20 years in the IT industry, working with global IT giants for some fortune 500 customers, he started exploring his other interests - the cultural & spiritual history of India and its great past of oneness. He utilized his free time in reading, listening, thinking, reconnecting with like-minded friends, and traveling to some spiritual places and ashrams. By God's grace he authored a book "Discovery of New India" in 2021, in which discuss some difficult to solve problems of our country, and suggested solutions. Motivated by the observation that those suggestions and solutions are being implemented, he got inspired to write this book. Through this book "2050 - India Turns 100", Vaibhav shares his vision for India, and encourages you to participate in building the India of your dreams